Problems!
Problems!

Problems! Problems!

Confessions of an Agony Aunt

VIRGINIA
IRONSIDE

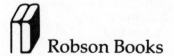

Robson Books

First published in Great Britain in 1991 by Robson
Books Ltd, Bolsover House, 5–6 Clipstone Street,
London W1P 7EB

British Library Cataloguing in Publication Data
Ironside, Virginia
 Problems! Problems!
 I. Title
 070.444

 ISBN 0 86051 755 1

Photoset in North Wales by
Derek Doyle & Associates, Mold, Clwyd.
Printed and bound in Great Britain by
WBC Print and WBC Bookbinders Ltd,
Bridgend, Mid-Glamorgan.

For Kate Ironside

Contents

It is a typical party. Imagine the scene. My neighbour has just had a new baby and her partner has thrown a party to celebrate. I arrive, fluffy teddy in hand, eager to chuck the little chap under the chin and join in all the coochie-coos. There is a general hubbub, and through the scrum I can see that everyone is happy. All the friends and relations are there. A Christmas tree glitters in a corner; the delicious smell of hot punch wafts across the cosy sitting room.

But just as I am about to plunge through the fray to deliver my gift, my way is barred by a big, beaming, red-faced man in a blazer.

'Brother-in-law,' says the Blazer, holding out his hand for a shake. 'Or I would be if they were married. I'm a something-in-law. Or perhaps a common-law brother-in-law. Let me get you a drink.'

'Thanks – I must just give this present to …'

'Are you local?' he says.

'Very. Just a few doors down,' I reply.

'Great night for a party,' he says, eyeing an open french window through which a gale is howling. 'Get everyone outside. Having a good time?'

'Yes.'

'So,' he says, quickly dispensing with the conversational foreplay as he steers me to a table covered in wine-boxes. 'And what do you do for a living?'

'I'm a journalist.'

'Oho! Better watch what I say, eh?'

'I'm not that kind of journalist,' I reply, rather stuffily. 'I also write books.' Should never have said I was a journalist.

Should have learnt by now.

'So what do you scribble, then? In your journalism?'

'Oh, this and that.'

'Come on,' says the Blazer. 'What do you do? Women's stuff? Political stuff?'

'I answer people's problems.'

I should have never said that. I should have ...

'Aha! The agony aunt! They told me about you!' The Blazer moves his eyes away from the blustery garden and full onto my face. His expression is pure victory. 'How absolutely fascinating!'

'It is. And what do you do?'

'You must get an awful lot of letters!'

'Yes, but what do you do?

'But isn't it terribly depressing?'

Sighing, I lean against the wall and begin. 'Not a bit,' I say, looking surreptitiously at my watch. The baby will still be around in an hour, surely. 'Get me a drink and let me explain.'

'Let Me Explain'

Whenever I say I couldn't bear to give up writing an agony column, few people can understand why. Indeed, most of them seem to think that being an agony aunt is rather trivial, a joke of a job. Wouldn't it be nicer, I see them thinking, in bubbles over their head, to be a feature-writer for *Harper's & Queen*? To write a biography of the Sitwells? To be an arts reviewer? To throw it all up and write best-sellers?

The answer is: no, it wouldn't. Because there's something immensely satisfying about being an agony aunt. I would hate *not* to be an agony aunt. I don't even care about the title. Some agony aunts insist on being called Problem Page Editors or Advice Columnists. Not me. You can call me what you like – ag aunt, auntie, sob sister – who cares? As long as I can do this peculiarly idiosyncratic job.

Ever since I was a child I've always loved agony columns. Mary Grant was the one I read most, my stepmother being a *Woman's Own* reader at the time. Indeed, my father was once up in arms about a reply that Mary Grant had written on her page – I think it was something about genetics and whether a white couple with a black ancestor could ever have a black child (or more probably, in those days, 'coal-black'). Always incensed by anything which was scientifically wrong, and genetics being a particular hobbyhorse of his, my father wrote to Mary Grant explaining, with the aid of elegantly-drawn diagrams, how her answer was not genetically possible. The result was that Angela Willans (who, at the time, it turned out, actually was 'Mary Grant', before she 'came out' and was allowed to use her real name) came to drinks with us to discuss the matter.

I remember sitting curled up in a chair, a rather sulky teenager, only present because I longed to have a peep at a real agony aunt. It's rather uncanny to find Angela now one of my agony aunt colleagues whom I particularly like and admire.

I first heard about the job when I was taken out to lunch by the assistant editor at *Woman*. I had just finished droning on about a few rather dreary possible freelance ideas when she called the lunch to an abrupt halt by asking for the bill before the coffee. She had to rush off back to the office, she said, because a drama had erupted minutes before she'd left. Anna Raeburn was leaving. They were desperate to find a replacement. I made polite noises about what a super job that would be for someone – and as I spoke, the assistant editor stared at me, waved away the man with the bill, ordered two coffees and another drink, stared at me intently and said: 'Do you really mean that?'

I couldn't imagine that she was serious. To me it was rather like saying, politely, that the Queen must have a very interesting job – and then to find yourself in line for the throne. I was overwhelmed at the idea of even being considered for such an exalted position.

The job offer came at a crucial time in my life. I had been a freelance journalist for years, had written a book, had worked as a rock columnist on the *Daily Mail* talking to people like the Beatles and the Rolling Stones (taking care I didn't faint with fan-worship halfway through the interviews); I'd reviewed television for the *Mail* and at the time I was writing columns for teenage magazines. But to add to all this, I was just emerging from a long period of depression. Several years had passed when I had considered suicide every single day. I was divorced with a small son, I felt totally inadequate, I constantly fell for unsuitable men. My mother,

Janey Ironside, a brilliant career woman who was Professor of Fashion at the Royal College of Art in the sixties and who had left my father and myself when I was fourteen, had lost her job by unwisely resigning on a matter of principle and, in between suicide attempts, had taken to the bottle in a big way. I had become so depressed I could hardly feel anything, even hunger.

Via several psychiatrists, I had been through courses of anti-depressants and tranquillizers, group therapy, psychotherapy, analysis, hypnotherapy – you name it and I'd either swallowed it or 'experienced the learning process' of it. At the time that I was lunching with the assistant editor, however, I was just starting to see a light at the end of the tunnel and was beginning to believe I had the answer to everyone's problems, evangelical about therapy and convinced I had something to offer troubled people. And I think it was this burning desire to spread the therapeutic word that must have convinced the editor that I was a good person for the job. (Of course, whether to admit to all this appalling nuttiness and misery in my past was another thing; I decided, eventually, to keep quiet about it. A history of acute depression might make one extremely well-qualified to be an agony aunt but the information could cut both ways.)

I need hardly say that in the years that have passed, I have stopped looking everything up in Freud and believing I can cure the world of its ills; my approach has become a lot more pragmatic and straightforward. Whether it's better or not, I don't know. But my feeling is that an agony aunt should be a friend – and a friend simply gives advice from the heart and the head, not from a book of theory.

People often ask me if I don't get fed up with people bearding me at parties (as apparently they do to doctors) and telling me their problems. In fact, the question most people ask me at parties is whether I get fed up with people bearding me at parties telling me their problems. And the answer is that they don't.

'Oh, no, I would never ask you about my problems,' says the Blazer, hastily. 'Or perhaps you could tell me how to make money without working for a living? Ha ha!' I fix him with a stony stare.

In fact, only a few close friends come to me with their problems and they come to me because they know me very well. I'm not a trained counsellor and it would be irresponsible of me to talk to perfect strangers about their problems – my strength is in writing and not in talking. There is a very good reason I am an agony aunt and not a psychologist or a counsellor – it is because primarily I'm a writer and journalist and I don't think I'd be any better at talking to people and counselling them than I think most psychologists or counsellors would be very good at answering people's letters in a newspaper. They would find themselves at sea. And anyway the answer 'Hmm. Yes, I'm here. I'm listening. And how do *you* feel about all this?' doesn't make a tremendously good read.

But isn't it depressing? Far from it. First of all, helping a person is rather like building a fire for someone who is very cold – while you're building it, a little bit of the heat comes your way as well. And then, if I come into the office feeling low and unloved, as everyone does from time to time, there's nothing that perks me up more than a pile of letters from people far, far more miserable, lonely and wretched than myself. Reading letters from readers who are trapped in intolerable situations and sometimes have no friends at all, is, while tragic and depressing in one sense, also a reminder to oneself of how very many blessings one has and how very lucky one is.

And lucky I am. I have a weekly column read by millions; I am reasonably well-known; I am one of a peculiarly exclusive and eccentric band – there are less than thirty agony aunts in England; on top of all this, I feel I'm doing something worthwhile and get a smug, warm, inner glow as I do it. Who wouldn't feel lucky?

*   *   *   *

The party is filling up even more. The Neighbour's Partner is handing round a plate of tiny footballs filled with squished-up cheese surrounded by bullet-hard, highly lacquered Japanese biscuits.

'My ex-wife used to read the problem pages,' *says the* Blazer. 'And so did my mother. And my grandmother. So I saw them occasionally.'

'Ah, you're talking about the agony column,' *says the* Neighbour's Partner. 'I knew you two would get on.'

'I've just filled him in on all the details,' *I say, putting my glass down and looking at my watch.* 'Good heavens! I must go and see your son! I've got a little prezzie for him....'

'Did you say your grandmother read the problem pages?' *says the Neighbour's Partner to the Blazer.* 'That's fascinating. I wonder what the problems were like then.'

'Oh, they must have been very uninteresting,' *says the* Blazer. ' "How do I keep my stays up?" Haha!'

' "How do I grow petunias!" ' *says the Neighbour's* Partner.

' "My best hat got spattered with rain!" ' *chortles the* Blazer. ' "I am beside myself!" '

I hesitate. 'It wasn't quite like that …' *I say, although I know I should keep my big mouth shut.* 'Problems were different in her day, but they weren't uninteresting. You,' *I say, nodding at the Blazer,* 'have already pinpointed a new problem by describing yourself as a "something-in-law". That shows a change in society's problems.'

'Something-in-law?' *says the Neighbour's Partner, looking rather crossly at the Blazer and withdrawing his plate of Japanese biscuits.* 'What on earth do you mean?'

'Well, if you were married, I'd be your brother-in-law, but as you're not, I …'

'It hardly matters,' I say, hastily. 'What I'm trying to say is that generally problems – and answers – were different from the ones I get today. But I must go and give your son his present.'

'Later,' says the Blazer, pouring me another glass of wine from a box. 'Tell me about problem pages in the past.'

'Different Problems, Different Answers'

I've always imagined agony aunts in the past to be rather stiff, spinster-like ladies without much experience of life. They would have blue rinses in their hair and wear white twin-sets and pearls and would call you 'my dear'.

These days, agony aunts are much more likely to be thirty-five year-old girls, with pink streaks in their hair rather than blue rinses, with perhaps a divorce and a nervous breakdown under their belts. The first agony aunt who ever existed was, surprise, surprise, a man. According to Robin Kent in her excellent book, *Agony*, (Star, 1987) one John Dunton was wandering round Lambeth in the late seventeenth century with a problem on his mind. He'd got himself embroiled in an extra-marital affair and needed anonymous help. When he struck on the idea of the agony column he cried, 'Gadzooks!' (or whatever people cried in those days) and announced he'd come up with a wheeze that he wouldn't swap for fifty guineas. This idea led to the birth of the first agony column in 1691 in his *Athenian Gazette*. Daniel Defoe was an agony uncle and, despite the fact that he had a long history of bankruptcy and fraud behind him, he was apparently extremely moralizing in his replies.

Looking back, it's easy to see that, as in everything else, there are fashions in problem-answering. The affectionate, friendly and loving feeling behind the replies may have been the same but the actual advice was vastly different. Take, for instance, this answer given in 1910 by the editress of the

7

Ladies' Home Paper in reply to a girl who signed herself 'Misery'.

> Dear Misery,
> Self-knowledge is half the battle. So cheer up, little Misery. Make up your mind that next time you write, your *nom de plume* will be 'Joy'. The way to clear a garden of weeds is to uproot them with a firm hand. And so, my dear girl, must you do with your faults. Pull them out at once, not by degrees, but with a good hearty tug. Remember also that there is One that is always ready help you; try to lean on Him a little more and when you are in doubt about anything just whisper to yourself 'What would He do?'

A charming answer – but I have to admit it's not one that I would use nowadays. I'd probably suggest that Little Misery went to see her GP and got herself some counselling and anti-depressants, since she was clearly suffering from depression.

In 1906 a woman complained to the editress of the *Girls' Home Paper* in 'Cosy Corner' that her husband often returned home from work very snappy, a problem not so uncommon today. She got this reply: 'You will be wiser next time, wee wife, and not grumble next time when your husband comes home tired after his day's work. Remember he has difficulties in town which a recital of yours at home will not lighten. You ought to be bright and cheery when he comes home – or be sure he will make a practice of spending his evenings elsewhere.'

In 1948 Mary Holmes, the agony aunt for *Lucky Star*, was giving virtually the same reply to a similar problem. She put it like this. 'Perhaps he really *is* very tired. He could easily be worried. Have you thought of sharing the gardening? Are you bright and welcoming when he returns home? I know this sounds as if I was putting everything onto you but men are rather like children in a way – they have to be fed and amused.'

A very different reply to a similar kind of problem came from Anna Raeburn, my predecessor at *Woman*. She snapped: 'Women don't have to submit to tyranny! Your husband may be a charming guest at a party but he sounds to me like a pain in the neck. If you pleased yourself more you might like yourself better instead of just trying to please your husband. Just for the record, *he* has the problem.'

Then there were those little paragraphs that so often appeared at the end of the agony column. The problem was never actually printed – all you saw was a cryptic note to Worried Blue-Eyes or Desperate of Dagenham, on the lines of: 'Do not on any account continue to do what you have described! You will go mad and your hair will fall out!' And one always wondered what on earth Worried Blue-Eyes was up to, and became panic-stricken that one might be doing the same thing, unwittingly, oneself. It was in these paragraphs that the Plain Brown Envelope so often featured. As a carpenter needs his saw and the water diviner his rod, so any self-respecting agony aunt in the forties and fifties needed the pile of Plain Brown Envelopes by her side. I often think how awful it would have been in those days if one was the mother of a daughter who received one of those Plain Brown Envelopes through the post. One would have been horrified – convinced that any material in such packaging must inevitably be exceptionally rude and disgusting.

For instance, in 1940 in *Silver Star*, Mary Mann wrote to Worried Girl: 'The contents of your letter are of rather too intimate a nature to reply to here so if you write to me privately, enclosing a plain brown stamped addressed envelope and giving fuller facts concerning what you fear, I shall be pleased to advise you accordingly.'

In 1939 Marion Dark of *Glamour* replied to a similar reader whose letter was clearly too risqué to publish: 'I'm glad you realize the foolishness of what you contemplated. Stick to the principles you know are right. I will send you a booklet called *Why are Sexual Relations Before Marriage*

Wrong. The price is 4 pence.' In 1943, four years later, in the same column, things had changed slightly. 'Read my booklet,' she wrote in the usual lone paragraph to another reader who had strayed from the path, 'entitled *Why are Sexual Relations Before Marriage* Definitely *Wrong*. It is priced 5d.'

Even morals were subject to inflation. Sex is always a tricky subject. In the past it was always thought it could never really be enjoyable before marriage – quite apart from being wrong – and, indeed, I'd say it *was* wrong in days when there was no contraception. But even in marriage, sex had its dangers then, according to some medical advisers. Once a night was considered far too much. 'The evidence that an almost nightly indulgence is kept of the pleasures of the marriage bed, shows in their lustreless eyes, their sodden and greasy faces and their trembling hands,' wrote an adviser to one of his sexier clients.

Another, quoted, like the last one, in *Dear Prudence* by Gerard Macdonald (Century, 1985), wrote: 'Some patients for years indulged in sexual intercourse as often as once in twenty-four hours and some would have indulged still oftener. Of course the result was premature decay and often Permanent Invalidism.'

According to Dr John Post, who researched a programme, *A Short History of the Cold Shower*, for Radio Four, one Sylvanus Stall, a doctor of divinity in the 1890s and the author of *What a Young Boy Ought to Know*, told his readers that 'After congress, the male loses his appetite. Great physical changes result. The skin which covers his shrunken body changes in colour, his nature becomes irritable and resentful and he indulges in fierce combat with his fellows.' In answer to a man who asked if he should renounce the pleasures of love when he was fifty, he replied: 'Assuming you want to stay alive, you should. After fifty years of age, a man of sense ought to renounce the pleasures of love. Each time he allows himself this gratification is a pellet of earth thrown upon his coffin.'

However, much later, in the forties when contraception was

just starting to be mentioned in the problem pages (though definitely not sex before marriage), it was dancing that was deemed to be dangerous by Evelyn Home. 'If you had seen the number of letters I have received which say: "I thought I loved my husband (or fiancé) until I met another man at a dance," you would not underestimate the problem,' she wrote in 1945.

Evelyn Home, my predecessor before Anna Raeburn, was and still is a splendid woman. The only thing is, she doesn't exist. She is actually a lady called Peggy Makins but she was obliged to change her name to Evelyn Home when she joined *Woman* as agony aunt in the thirties. The idea was dreamt up by a middle-European psychologist on the run from Nazi Germany, who argued that the name 'Eve' summed up 'woman' as temptress and seductress (though Adam and Evelyn doesn't sound quite right for the inmates of the Garden of Eden), and that 'Home' evoked the housewife at the sink and the cooker. In vain did Peggy protest that Evelyn is just as commonly used as a man's name as a woman's – and that in most places north of Buckinghamshire the name 'Home' is pronounced 'Hume'.

People often ask me if my name is invented and, thinking about it, I can just imagine a psychologist rustling it up on the grounds that 'Virginia' has sexual implications while at the same time showing responsibility in the days of Aids, and 'Ironside' is the assertive career woman, the working woman of today. Anna Raeburn was one of the first to use her real name – which perhaps said more about women's status than any replies which advocated women's liberation. It emphasized that this woman really was an individual in her own right and not just some fantasy dreamt up by a psychologist.

But emancipation had hardly raised its head in the forties when Miss Nell St John Montague, writing for *Lucky Star*, answered a letter from a man about his wife who wanted to do war work in 1941, like her neighbour. He wrote: 'This neighbour was a quiet little woman before she went out to work but now you would not know her. She has lost her quietness and is most aggressive. Also she walks about in bright-coloured velvet trousers and her husband is no longer master in his own house. I am devoted to my wife but will war work have this effect upon her?'

In her reply, Miss Nell St John Montague commented, incredulously: 'I don't think your neighbour could really be doing serious work; otherwise she would not have behaved as she has done.'

In 1894 the idea of a working woman was even more appalling. Walter Heape, also quoted in *Dear Prudence*, wrote in a book on preparation for marriage: 'Working women so sorely affect the Natural Functions of their Sex that, with the exception of a small proportion of them, they can never wholly Regain the Conditions necessary in order to discharge the Duties of Maternity in a manner which is easy to themselves or satisfactory to their child.'

Women were not expected to stand up for themselves at all. In 1910 a woman wrote to *Woman's World* with a tragic tale:

I have three children but two of them are not with me as I left my husband two years ago. He lost two good situations through drink and dishonesty and the year I had my last baby he was very unkind to me. I got desperate and meant to leave him and take my children with me but my mother could not take me in with my three children so they got me away by myself. I went back the next day but he would not allow me to speak at all as his sisters were making arrangements to get the children into a home and they have been in one ever since. However, my heart was so sore that I stole my eldest girl from him and have been working for her this year and a half now. He has got nothing particular to do all this time and his sisters keep him. If he gets a situation, would you advise me to go back to him? Nearly everyone says no but I cannot live without my little ones as my heart is so sore when I get see them and have to leave them in the care of others.

This poor creature got the reply:

> Certainly you must go back, dear sister. You made a fatal mistake in leaving the man you had vowed to cherish, to love, for better for worse. You cannot – you must not – evade your matrimonial bargain in this way. Besides, there is only one person who can help this man to reform and become a changed character and that is yourself, his wife, the mother of his children! ... It will be a hard and thankless task but, dear sister, it is your duty – and duties cannot be avoided. Don't think of past wrongs and grievances, don't nag and above all, don't talk of your husband's faults to outsiders ... love him and be sure that your love will win from him a respect that will probably lead to better times ... [etc, etc.]

Today I would certainly advise this battered wife to contact a refuge for advice – and give her husband an ultimatum: that either he sought help for his drinking or the marriage was over. (Although alcohol was considered an evil, little was known about its effects – and in 1915 when Lloyd George called for higher duties on spirits, the Hon Member for South East Cork complained that his constituents needed whisky for women in childbirth – not to mention for those in the workhouses – 'to keep alive the poor creatures whose stomachs cannot bear food.')

Certainly girls were never encouraged to be forward. In 1930 when a girl wrote to *Girl's Friend* saying she wanted to know better a boy she'd been introduced to, Ruby Royston, the agony aunt, wrote back: 'I'm afraid there is nothing you can do, Sylvia, without appearing cheap. You must wait for him to ask you out.'

In 1978, on the other hand, when a girl asked Irma Kurtz a similar problem in *Cosmopolitan*, she got the reply: 'Ask him out. If he rejects you, suffer a little and then wait until your heart beats hard for someone else. After all, men have always risked rejection and now that we're "liberated" it's our turn.'

The war produced its own special problems – like the one

from the girl who wrote to Evelyn Home: 'My boyfriend is a conscientious objector. My father says he is being cowardly and unmanly (though he has volunteered for stretcher-bearing or mine-sweeping) and has ordered me to give him up ... Am I being unpatriotic in associating with this boy?' Evelyn Home, a Quaker herself, replied kindly:

> My dear, you have asked me a question which is quite impossible for anyone to settle for anyone else. Perhaps some conscientious objectors are cowards; quite often they are as brave as their fellow men. Mine-sweeping is just as dangerous as piloting a fighter aeroplane.... Most of us believe that if the country is in need it is up to every man to fight for her, if fighting is the only thing which will save her. Conscientious objectors think that fighting or violence is never justified. I cannot possibly go into my personal views on the subject and I am afraid you will have to make your own decision.

Another area of change has been in race relations. Someone wrote to Leonora Eyles in 1943 at *Woman's Own* asking if she could be friends with the black American soldiers on the local US air base. This is the reply she got: 'Personally, I would be friends with them but I am a middle-aged married woman. The only thing is that it would not be a close friendship that might lead to romance. It is by no means a matter of them being inferior, but different.' Were I to write anything like that now the Commission for Racial Equality would be down on me like a ton of bricks, not to mention the National Union of Journalists.

It's all a far cry from 1984, when Marje Proops in the *Daily Mirror* replied curtly to a young girl who had married an Indian and whose parents now snubbed them. 'When people are as ignorantly prejudiced as your parents seem to be, they aren't likely to listen to reason or understand anything about the real world.'

Class was a much bigger problem in the past than it is today. In 1925 *Eve's Own Stories* had a wonderful male agony uncle called Old Solomon, a chap who signed himself: 'Cheerily yours, your bachelor friend.'

A reader wrote to him: 'I am very worried about my best friend who has recently become engaged to a fellow who's certainly "one of the best" but lacks education or the position in life of my friend and of her parents. She has confided in me that although she really loves him she fears his lack of polish will come between them. I have met this boy myself and while he is undoubtedly clever and is doing well, I found him careless in his speech and, I'm afraid I must say, a little common in his manner and dress.'

I'm glad to say that Old Solomon gave quite jolly and friendly advice in the circumstances; I would have been more inclined to give this girl a verbal clout on the ear. 'If the man loves the girl and realizes that she is socially his superior,' he wrote, 'he will do all in his power to better himself so as to make his wife proud of him in every way.'

Other agony uncles were Charlie Strong in *My Paper* (1915) who signed himself 'Your true pal' or 'Your old pal'; and in the thirties there was a pipe-smoking character called Nigel Mansfield who set himself up in *Glamour* as 'OUR LOVE EXPERT – he will help you and tell you how to be happy in love.'

Agony aunts have always tended to be middle-class and sometimes sickeningly so, but surely Peg's Mother takes the middle-class biscuit. Introducing her in *Peg's Companion*, in 1921, Peg, the editor, wrote: 'I am going to share my mother with you girls. She will help you as she has helped me.'

Enter Peg's mother:

Dear All of You,

Although I've never really met any of you, I seem to know many of you through my girl Peg and when she came to me with her chums – as she speaks of you to me – I was delighted ... Peg and I love the twilight and it is then we get our 'comfy cosy talks' as we call them, I in my big armchair, which she bought me as a Christmas present, she on her 'humpty' cuddled up against my knees like she used to do as a little girl ... Every evening when the gloaming slips into dusk, I shall be waiting for you, dear girls, and one after another I want you to come into my room where I'm waiting for our twilight talk.

Yuk!

Hand in hand with the obsession with class was an obsession with etiquette and what was right, nice and proper and 'done' (as opposed to 'not done') and whether the neighbours would look down on certain practices and so on. I sometimes wonder what those old-fashioned agony aunties would have made of a problem sent to Angela Willans of *Woman's Own*. In 1980 she got a letter of the kind with which all present-day agony aunts are all too familiar. It's a new social problem and it's a tricky one. 'Because my parents are divorced, I'm paying for arranging my wedding and my grandfather will give me away. I'm in a panic, though, about the right way to sit everyone at the church and the reception, especially as the guests will include my mother's boyfriend, his relatives and my stepbrother and half-sister.'

In the thirties and forties there was a fashion for handwriting experts and astrologists who often doubled up as agony aunts. For instance, in 1940 Madame Sunya of *Peg's Paper* received a letter from a girl: 'I have been out with many boys but the affairs have never come to anything. They seem attracted to me but the attraction never lasts. Last year I met an airman but he has gone out of my life owing to a misunderstanding.' Her answer was: 'Don't despair, for your real happiness is now very close to you. There is a man in a blue uniform who will come to mean a lot to you. It is a dark blue and not a light blue one and he comes from across the water to you.'

Many problems change simply because laws have changed. For instance, homosexuality was against the law in the thirties and in 1936 Miss Nell St John Montague was forced to answer this sad letter in a heart-rendingly negative way. A woman wrote: 'I'm afraid I have an exceedingly handsome son of 16 but he has made friends with a young man of 23 who adores my son and says if my son were a girl he would marry him. Of course if my son were a girl I wouldn't mind so much.' Miss Nell St John Montague wasn't able to refer this lady, as I would, to a self-help group for parents of homosexual children. She could only reply: 'I think you should get your husband to talk to your son very kindly. Just point out to him that such a friendship is not right and will only cause him to be looked down upon. Please write to me again.'

Of course, attitudes to homosexuality have changed drastically. In fact, Dr David Delvin, author of many sex books, has said: 'Whenever I used to write the statement that is currently fashionable, that no one is wholly homosexual or heterosexual and we are all a little bit of each, I would get absolutely outraged letters that would go like this: "Dear Dr Delvin, What rubbish. I personally am entirely heterosexual. Stop standing up for the these goddam pooves and fairies. Yours sincerely, Disgusted of Tunbrige Wells." ' But he says that now, if he makes the same statement, he's more likely to get a letter along these lines: 'Dear Doc. I take real exception to what you say. Personally I am a hundred per cent gay and there is not a drop of heterosexual blood in my body. How dare you suggest otherwise! Yours furiously, Indignant of Hampstead.'

And with the advent of AIDS the mood may be changing again. Indeed, the introduction of Clause 28 was a sad sign that the clock may be turning back.

Sex queries, as we've seen, were not usually discussed on the page. Certainly sex before marriage was strongly disapproved of. When a girl in the fifties had 'given in' (as it was then called) to her boyfriend, she wrote to Evelyn Home saying she was 'terribly disappointed. I experienced none of the joy and thrill that is supposed to come with intercourse....

We have both been very sad about this and my boy gets awfully nervy and miserable about it … I'm afraid I shall be just the same when we're married.'

Evelyn Home replied: 'The privileges of matrimony can very rarely be truly enjoyed by those who have not been properly married. If you were married, in your own home, with privacy and the opportunity to learn tenderness as well as to give way to passion, you would find the utmost pleasure in the intimate relationship. Your boy has no need to work himself up into such a state of uncontrolled nerves. He should find strength in the thought that you are preserving an infinitely precious thing that will forever brighten your life together after you are married.' She now says, 'I imagine nowadays the security of the Pill can take the place of the security of marriage. Not that feeling secure necessarily produces sexual pleasure, but it should help.'

The time that the social climate really started to change in a big way was in the sixties – but as late as 1960 Marje Proops was faced with an impossible dilemma, even for her. (Marje Proops is, of course, the doyenne of agony aunts. Observant readers will have noticed from her column photograph in the *Daily Mirror* that the health-conscious Marje has swapped her distinctive cigarette and holder for a pen in recent years, but her style continues extraordinarily fresh, original and quirky. One person who signed herself 'Over Forty' got a reply from Marje charmingly addressed: 'Dear Over'.)

The question was from a woman called Desperate who wanted to live with a man who wasn't divorced but was separated and living apart from his wife. But Marje, even in 1960, was completely stumped. 'Usually I'm not afraid to face up to an issue or reluctant to pass an opinion but here is one time when I can't say: "Yes, go ahead" or "Forget this man." Here is one time when Dear Marje is going to appeal to you, Dear Reader, for help. If a woman like Desperate came to YOU for advice and help, what would you say to her? Write and tell me the advice you would pass on to her.'

You would have thought that at the beginning of the permissive sixties there would not be much difficulty in deciding what the answer should be, but in fact readers wrote in their thousands to answer the question: 'Is love worth this sacrifice?' with: 'No, Desperate!' – 'The stigma would be too great to bear' – 'When the first novelty and bliss begin to fade you are left with the guilt and the humiliation' – 'The sham wedding ring is a constant reminder of the fact there never was and never will be a wedding' – 'In the end she will hate him as much as she hates herself ...'

Marje seemed rather astounded by this reaction and wrote to the reader, with typical kindness, 'Whatever you do, here's wishing you luck and happiness in the future.'

When I got to *Woman* in 1978, I was astonished to find just how little had changed since the old days. The leaflets had barely altered since the thirties. There were leaflets entitled *Glove-Making* and *Etiquette*. There was even one on *Laying a Table* – 'Where table-mats are to be used to protect a polished surface, these can be laid at each place ready for the plate to be put on them,' it advised, and 'At breakfast one needs racks for toast and a deep plate with spoon for cereal if this is to be served.' There was a leaflet called *Guest in the House* – in the bedroom there should be '... hangers, shoe trees and a waste paper basket. An ashtray for smokers and a tin of biscuits for those who wake ravenous in the night.' And as for washing up – 'A debatable point. Should the hostess accept a guest's offer to help? Many people prefer their guests to have a completely restful time. But if the offer is accepted, freshly laundered tea towels please!' There was also rather a good one called *Manners for Men* which included tips on how to behave at table. 'Pâté is balanced on a piece of toast, not spread –' (Cripes, I've been doing it wrong all my life, then) – and 'avocado pear comes in halves with stone removed. Pour sauce or dressing in the hollow. Hold pear on plate, eat with a small spoon.' And finally:

'When an engagement is announced, remember that you congratulate the man but not the girl. Whatever you may know to the contrary, convention has it that he has done all the chasing and won the "prize".' Whatever you know to the contrary! Cheek!

There were also no sex leaflets at *Woman* except a few yellowing sheets referred to euphemistically as 'Leaflet A'.

It was not until around 1970 that issues began to be treated a lot more liberally and openly. *Rave* magazine had an agony column called 'Lifeline' and in 1971 Jenny Clark answered a letter from a girl going round with a drop-out drug addict with: 'Drop the drop-out. Fast.'

Pregnant girls with fears that too much LSD might affect the foetus, homosexuals and girls in search of abortions were all answered frankly and fearlessly in *Rave*. (Indeed it was in *Rave* that I broke new ground by writing of a girl, in a fictional serial called 'Ronnie, the Diary of a Rave Girl', who slept with her boyfriend before she was married. I responsibly took her to the Family Planning Clinic first, however.)

By now the idea of psychiatry was becoming more acceptable and even in the fifties there was occasional advice to try it. One reader was asked to suggest her husband made an appointment with a psychiatrist because of his behaviour which, as the reader herself pointed out, 'all started at home in his own childhood'. This was all deep stuff compared to the 'remember you are a wife, my dear' attitude of former years. However, it was probably Anna Raeburn, who came to *Woman* in 1974 from *Forum* magazine, who gave the door to the permissive society the biggest kick of all. Suddenly we found exactly what was in those Plain Brown Envelopes.

'Penises and vaginas are not meant to be controlled so they don't have climaxes. Either do it or don't do it, but stop messing about,' she wrote in answer to one letter, mentioning in the popular press those two words that had, until now, been taboo.

Other letters mentioned sex more frankly, too. For instance: 'I was a virgin when I got married. My husband thinks that I was not because I did not bleed when we first had intercourse....' Or: 'Is this love? I really can't believe, as a mature intelligent woman of 40 that I need to write this letter. I run two church groups, am well-respected and admired by most people ... I haven't felt passionately about my husband so our sex-life hasn't meant a great deal to me. But, three weeks ago my eldest son brought home a friend, slightly older than himself – 21 – and, bluntly, I fancied him.'

By 1991 Marje was replying to a letter from a fifty-one-year-old man who wrote because, after ten years as a celibate widower and despite being able to masturbate successfully, he now found himself impotent with his new wife, who affectionately called him 'her darling droopy'. In her answer, Marje, as usual, pulled no punches: 'Let's be explicit and not mince words – your penis has forgotten how to perform one of its main functions. Well, it hasn't forgotten entirely because it springs to life when it and you are alone together enjoying private pleasures. But when faced with your partner, you become so tense that your little friend can't stand up to her expectations and your hopes ... I realize your shyness was why you decided to remain anonymous, but by now you must have realized that words like erection don't embarrass me.'

Answers differ so enormously over the years that in the end one's often left wondering which answers are actually 'right'. But the fashions in advice are much the same as fashions in clothes, and what may seem to us today so incredibly advanced, liberal and mightily understanding of the human condition, will probably look fantastically quaint and peculiar in fifty years' time. And although old problem-page answers can sometimes look rather silly, they were right at the time.

When *Woman* was fifty years old in 1987, I had the rather smart-arsed idea of doing a feature that would consist of one page of Evelyn Home's problems with her replies; on the facing page would be the same problems with my brilliant up-to-date answers. The idea came to nothing because of course when I searched through the files I couldn't find any of Evelyn Home's replies that weren't eminently kind and sensible. There were none of those 'Why not wear sexy underwear to greet your husband when he comes home?' answers. There were no exhortations to readers telling them to pull themselves together or turn to God. There was nothing about marriage being for ever or telling women not to go to work.

And I hope that, fifty years on, something will come across from our answers today – something behind the quirky fashions of the nineties, fashions we are now too close to be able to pinpoint. And I hope that people who look back on today's problem page answers will be able to see what comes over loud and clear in those problem page answers in the past – love, care and kindness.

*   *   *   *

'And now,' I say, 'I must let you go. I've been talking non-stop.' I've noticed the Blazer's eyes glazing over, particularly after my final homily, and he says: 'I must go and circulate. But don't go away! I'll be back!' But his voice says he probably won't be back. He disappears into a crowd of jabbering faces.

'Now, I'm just dying to see the baby,' I say to the Neighbour's Partner. 'I saw yours was completely bald – like all the best babies.'

The Neighbour's Partner glows. 'I'm afraid he's just being fed upstairs,' he says, sadly. 'But in the meantime I must just do the canapé rounds.'

'Canapés? You call those canapés?' says a motherly woman, bustling up. 'I told you....'

'Mum!' says the Neighbour's Partner. 'Let me introduce you both! This is....'

'I know,' says the Motherly Woman. 'The agony aunt! I've been just dying to meet you! Now you be away with those biscuits. Horrible hard things, break your teeth, should have let me do you some sandwiches, but she insisted ... Now, do tell me all. Firstly – don't you find people are always coming up to you at parties and telling you their problems?'

'No....'

'Oh how odd. Now tell me,' asks the Motherly Woman, settling herself on the arm of a nearby chair. 'This is what I can never understand. Speaking personally, I could never write to a problem page. Surely,' she says, 'it's only very stupid people who write in?'

'Surely It's Only Very Stupid People Who Write In?'

Agony aunts' post-bags range from around 10,000 to 50,000 letters a year – but the number varies according to the time of year. The figures tend to be low in the summer – if it's a good summer, that is – and then they start to rise during the autumn. Just before Christmas they drop drastically – because presumably everyone's frantically preparing for Christmas and imagining they're going to have a brilliant few days with their families. But just after Christmas the figures suddenly zoom up again – because perhaps not everyone *has* had a very jolly Christmas with their families. No speaks, rowing etc. And given that the expectation of a family Christmas being wonderful is so high, it's only very rarely that the actual holiday measures up to the fantasy. Often, indeed, far from Christmas being a time when families' links and ties are established and strengthened, the cracks and splits and disagreements actually show up to a greater degree than usual and, particularly after a few drinks, it may suddenly become abundantly clear why your brother and sister-in-law are heading for a divorce or why your father loathes his mother-in-law's guts and so on.

During this, the Motherly Woman, who has been about to help herself to more wine, changes her mind and switches to orange juice. She is looking shocked. She tries to protest but

I've started so I'll finish.

The figures level out around January and February and then start to rise again during the spring – when, interestingly enough, the suicide rate goes up as well. No one knows exactly why but some doctors say that a change of light patterns makes some people depressed – which is why people often feel depressed in the autumn, too. And one can also understand people feeling depressed in the spring if they're a bit low, because what they see happening outside in nature only contrasts with and therefore heightens their own feelings of unhappiness. The buds are budding, the bees are buzzing and the butterflies are flitting from bush to bush, as PG Wodehouse might say, and young lovers are flaunting their happiness in the sunshine as the birds start singing and preparing their nests; if you're feeling the tiniest bit low during the beginning of the new life of the year, all this wretched burgeoning can make your own gloom seem far, far worse.

Why do people write to a problem page? A lot of us would rather die than put all our private thoughts, plus our names and addresses, on paper, and then pop them in the post to a complete stranger. How can people be sure that their letters aren't opened by secretaries who pass them round the office screaming with laughter? How do they know the letters will be kept confidential? The truth is they don't – and it shows what an extraordinary amount of trust people have in agony aunties that they will write very intimate things to them – things which are often shocking, libellous, not to mention sometimes illegal.

My feeling is that most of us are happy to talk over our problems face to face with a relative or friend. We meet for coffee and we tell all. The friend, ideally, will be not only sympathetic but also have some good impartial advice – and in return we listen to our friends' problems when they're down.

Some people don't like doing this. They feel shy when eyeball to eyeball with someone, even someone they know and trust. And I can sympathize. You only have to catch your friend's eye as it tries to peep at the clock, to spot a yawn being stifled or to see her eyes glaze over with boredom – and then you hurry your problem up or try to make light of it, for her sake. You're still left with the problem, however.

There's also the trouble with weakness. Many's the time I've burst into tears while telling a friend a problem. I don't exactly relish it; I would much prefer not to. Which is why I, like many other people, prefer talking about problems on the telephone rather than face to face. I don't know why it is – it just feels more comfortable to me, and from the amount of time some people spend on the phone moaning to each other, it seems that I'm not alone. The other thing about the phone is that it's easier to catch someone; if you have to meet someone, you may have to make an appointment for lunch or tea by which time the crisis may be over. You can get instant help on the phone – and if the other person is bored, raising their eyebrows despairingly or making yapping signals with their hands at other people in the room, at least you can't see it.

It's people who prefer the phone to a face-to-face discussion who may find the Samaritans a good source of sympathy.

Then there are those who like to go and see their doctor or a counsellor about their problems. They see these people as fairly remote, people who might know the rest of their family but not intimately, professionals who only see a certain side of their lives, who are relatively distant figures of authority. The men in white coats may even be seen, and experienced, as magical figures.

And then there's another group of people who like to write letters. There's a great deal to be said for writing letters. Who hasn't written to 'Dear Diary' in times of stress? I have bookfuls of the stuff written between the ages of fifteen and thirty, and more self-indulgent, boring, wretched and tragic documents I have yet to read. But they were therapeutic. And up to a point writing to an agony aunt fulfils the Dear Diary function. You can write as long as you like, and moan to your heart's content. It's not like talking on the phone when someone can say, all too easily, 'Sorry, the potatoes are burning' or 'The bell's just gone.' And of course one of the reasons people write in is because they know they will get a personal reply back, even if their letter doesn't appear on the page.

When you write a letter, too, you leave all your extraneous baggage behind. It is an 'essential' way of communicating. When I read a letter from a reader I have absolutely no idea really what sort of person he or she is. I can analyze the handwriting, look at the quality of the paper, ponder over the spelling and the phrasing, but these are the only tiny clues I have to a reader's place in society. So our communication is unhampered by body language, by the instant assumptions one makes about other people on account of their clothes, accent, eyes, cleanliness, physical attractiveness and so on. There is a purity about the pain that a face-to-face counsellor might have to burrow deep to find.

Sometimes people write because they obviously like the sort of replies I give. I often wish that GPs had to present themselves as defencelessly to prospective patients as agony aunts do to their readers. I'd like to go my public library and get a video of all the GPs in my neighbourhood speaking to different patients (or even actors if it had to be). Then I could choose whose list I wanted to be on.

With agony aunts you never rush into the unknown. There's no risk. Readers can watch an agony aunt week after week, tripping, making a fool of herself, revealing all kinds of prejudices and flaws, but hopefully sometimes hitting the nail on the head – and all before they decide to confide in her. They often write in saying, 'Dear Virginia, I am writing to you because you always seem so down-to-earth and sensible.' That always made me glow – until I opened the odd letter to Angela Willans on *Woman's Own* whose post had been wrongly directed to me (we shared the same office building) and read that other readers had written exactly the same to her! And when Claire Rayner joined *Woman*, some of her post, when addressed simply to the Problem Page, would stray my way accidentally, and I'd open it up to find: 'Dear Claire, I'm writing to you because you're so down-to-earth and sensible.'

Claire Rayner believes people write in to us because 'we're like the old woman down at the end of the village, the one who knows a little bit about herbs and who's delivered the most number of children without them dying'. Irma Kurtz, who writes for *Cosmopolitan*, feels much the same. 'The role we play is the rabbi's wife in the kitchen court. While the rabbi and all the men are talking about how the world's going to end and how it began, the woman, the rabbi's wife, is in the kitchen talking to the other women about things like the eldest son, what is he going to do and so on. And people write to us also because they see us as a kind of white witch. Seven tenths of the people who write to me want a love potion. I'm the little old lady at the bottom of the lane and they come down saying: "Can I have a potion to sprinkle on his coffee?" But this old woman usually has a certain sense of things. She knows what strange plants grow in the forest and also knows quite a bit about human nature. But of course it doesn't mean our own lives are perfect or that we're calm and sorted out ourselves.'

Some people write because they've either been to their doctor and received no joy or because they daren't go to their doctor for fear they'll be laughed out of the surgery. I have a standard letter on how to change your doctor and I'm always appalled at how unhelpful some GPs can be – and how people feel they have no power over changing them. It's true that if they're stuck in a small village there may be no choice, but in a town they can always chop and change. And yet too many people see GPs as gods rather than public servants. And the GPs I hear about in readers' letters (the dissatisfied clients) seem to do little to persuade them otherwise.

'My doctor just told me to pull myself together' – 'My doctor asked what was I complaining about – he said I should be happy that my husband doesn't beat me or get drunk or have affairs' – 'My doctor is getting fed up with me' – 'My doctor said I should wear sexy nighties to turn my husband on' – 'My doctor was furious when my husband and I told him we wanted help for my husband's drinking. He said no way was my husband an alcoholic and simply gave him anti-depressants' – 'I daren't go to my doctor because he is a man/ very brusque/ I'd feel silly wasting his time' – 'My doctor says at my age, fifty-five, I shouldn't expect to get an erection'....

These are all typical comments from my mailbag. (It does seem to me that though most doctors are undoubtedly helpful with problems like these, an awful lot do not like talking about sex or drink because it often reminds them of their own failings!)

Some people, of course, write because they're just incredibly lonely and don't have anyone in the world to confide in. It's not that difficult to be completely friendless. Let's say a girl in the North marries against her parents' wishes and comes to live down South. She has no friends and no relatives nearby – and when her husband turns into a jealous and possessive man who refuses to allow her out, it's not surprising to discover she has no one to turn to. You don't even have to be trapped by a violent husband to be friendless. You may not know how to make friends, you may be terribly shy, you may live in a remote village.

I remember passing by a hoarding for a magazine which read: 'He was Best Man 65 times!' Tantalized by the headline, I bought the magazine to find out who this popular chap was – only to find that this was a guy who earned his living hiring himself out to couples who had no friends *at all* to give them away at their wedding. The fact that sixty-five couples were so friendless they were reduced to hiring a best man really brought home to me again how very lonely some people are.

People often write with fears that they feel other people would laugh at if they confided in them. For instance, a common problem I get is: 'I'm sure I can't get pregnant because when we make love my husband's semen runs out of me when I stand up.' It only takes a line to explain that this happens to everyone – in fact it is such a common query I have a standard letter on it. They can also ask me all kinds of silly things like whether masturbation really makes you blind, whether they could get pregnant even though they've had a hysterectomy, and so on. As Miss Lonelyhearts found, in the 1933 novel of the same name by Nathanael West (Penguin), 'The letters were no longer funny. He could not go on finding the same joke funny thirty times a day for months on end. And on most days he received more than thirty letters, all of them alike, stamped from the sough of suffering with a heart-shaped cookie knife.' While some letters can't fail to bring a smile, sometimes even prompting a howl of black-humoured laughter because the problem is so ghastly there's no other reaction available except for jumping off a bridge oneself in horror at the human condition, no agony aunts would reply by laughing at a reader's problem.

But I think that most people write to us because other sources have failed them. Not only with advice, support, love and sympathy, but with information; information about self-help groups, books, associations, health resource centres, counselling services. Every time I get a letter from someone who needs information I wonder why they haven't been able to get it elsewhere.

The jealousy with which information and further help for needy people is guarded by professionals is something I feel immensely angry about. I recently attended a forum organized by the Patients' Association. The theme was how

GPs could help their patients more and where did information come into all this. It all got off to a roaring start, with a delightful GP giving a talk and quoting the story of one of his patients who had been down to casualty. 'And what did they say?' he asked her when she visited him later at the surgery.

'Oh, nothing,' she replied.

'Nothing?'

'No.'

'But why ... surely?'

'It's that oaf, you see.'

The GP racked his brain for which particular consultant she could be referring to, when she added: 'That Hippocratic oaf, which means doctors aren't allowed to tell nobody nothing!'

This telling story was recounted to illustrate how secretive doctors are with their patients and the GP continued his amusing talk with anecdotes about his patients, including a long-term one with asthma, and information he'd given and so on.

Problem-page editors had been invited to this forum to put forward any good wheezes we had about information and the patient, and what astonished all of us was how resistant everyone on the medical side was to the idea of giving of information at all.

Couldn't GPs have leaflets on stock topics like cystitis, thrush, blood pressure and so on? Oh no. Children would snatch them in bunches and tear them up.

Couldn't they site the leaflet rack higher up on the wall? It would be difficult, and anyway patients wouldn't like to take leaflets called VD in front of other people. (This was from one of the medical mentors. The initials VD have not been used to describe sexually transmitted diseases for decades. The leaflet issued by the Health Education Authority on the subject is simply called *Guide to a Healthy Sex-life*, but perhaps he'd never seen a copy of this highly informative booklet which is available to anyone free. If, that is, they know where to get it from. Which is, of course, unlikely.) Anyway, no one liked the idea of too many bits of paper.

So what about just giving patients the names of an organization where they could find out more about their illness, if it was appropriate? No, it would take too long checking each organization; they spring up like mushrooms, some aren't any good.

So, what about just having a list of the basic big organizations like the MS Society, Mencap, British Heart Foundation, Age Concern, Disabled Living Foundation and hundreds of other highly respected concerns and charities that have been going for years? Oh, patients wouldn't like to have bits of paper thrust at them, they'd feel fobbed off. And it would be too difficult to look them up each time.

What about simply encouraging GPs to possess *The Health Directory*, published by the Patients' Association, and having it around so that they could easily look up whatever organization they wanted? The answer to this, believe it or not, was: 'Good idea. Why don't you recommend your readers to ask for *The Health Directory* when they see their doctors to encourage doctors to get hold of it!'

By this time some of the audience (particularly, interestingly, those who were connected with health) were getting in on the act. One person had heard of someone who had picked up a leaflet about breast screening in a Citizen's Advice Bureau and got the wrong end of the stick and become anxious. This was a good reason, she warned, to be chary of giving out information to anyone who couldn't properly understand it. (As Deidre Sanders of the *Sun* whispered to me, she'd never heard of anyone dying of reading a leaflet. As it is, most leaflets produced by national organizations are in words of one syllable, exceptionally vague and use words like 'medication' instead of listing specific drugs, and so on.)

The morning wore on and the agony aunts and advisers became more and more astonished (this one increasingly enraged) at the response of the professionals. Could it be that they were jealously hugging their secrets to themselves? That they didn't want to give too much information to the patients in case they somehow escaped from them? Or were they frightened that their patients might start to know too much about their own illnesses? After all, doctors are rather like agony aunts – we deal with the minor injuries and diseases but send people on to specialists because we can't know about everything. I could only conclude that an enormous number of doctors don't want their patients to know too much. They see it as a threat.

The final crazy suggestion came from one member of the panel who tried to compromise between the GPs and the agony aunts with: 'What about a computer that patients could access their questions into and would give them the answers?'

A computer is a machine that can only be worked by people either brave enough to ask or who know already; it frightens off anyone who is shy, nervous or too old to want to understand.

In all, I came away from that meeting feeling tremendously depressed. And particularly depressed to find that when I asked the GP whether he had ever given the address of the Asthma Society to the long-term patient he mentioned who suffered with it, he replied, 'No.' And yet when I mentioned the Asthma Society in a tiny answer on the page it received 5,000 enquiries in a week. And a recent article quoted a consultant as saying that: 'Doctors who do not recognize asthma or *who do not explain it adequately to patients* bear some of the responsibility for the 2,000 deaths from asthma a year.'

I make no excuses for banging on about the importance of information. I suffer myself with ulcerative colitis and until I arrived at *Woman* I never knew there was a self-help group with an informative newsletter and helpful leaflets on the subject. Neither my GP nor my consultant had ever mentioned it to me. I never thought to ask. And I would have felt shy asking, as it would have sounded as if I hadn't trusted them. And yet it's only as a result of reading all the Society's material, particularly their booklet on drugs, that I have managed to get my medication changed completely and feel vastly better.

And the argument that doctors need to protect a kind of mystery in order to be able to cure patients, by using the magic of the white coat, simply doesn't preclude the giving of information. A doctor can give the address of the Chest, Heart and Stroke Association to a patient and still exude intangible and magical healing powers. The giving of information and the magic are not mutually exclusive.

The Motherly Woman is trying to get a word in edgeways. But I am watching the Neighbour's Partner, now touring the room with a pile of tiny sausages that exude a tantalizing smell. I hope against hope he will come our way. I try to catch his eye, but the Motherly Woman is speaking.

'Did you say there was a self-help group for people who suffer from ulcerative colitis?' she says. 'Isn't that something like Crohn's Disease? My neighbour suffers.'

'The society covers both,' I say. 'I can – and will – give you the address. Hold on a second.' I scrabble in my bag as the sausages pass by and hear the Motherly Woman say: 'No thanks, dear, figure to watch!'

Sighing, I write out the address and then prepare to give chase to the vanishing plate, but the Motherly Woman is talking again.

'What I want to know,' she says, 'is how many of the letters are hoaxes. How do you know they're not invented?' I temporarily give up the idea of sausages, to reply.

Most people seem to think that the letters that come in are

so extraordinary that the vast majority must be hoaxes. They're not. Agony aunts learn to spot hoaxes. Many of the letters I get are often pages and pages long, sometimes whole pads of Basildon Bond with the glue still intact at the top. The readers will write on one side of every sheet of the pad and then turn the pad over and write on the back of every sheet. One letter, on computer print-out paper, was twenty-five feet long. Marje once had a letter seventy-two pages long.

A hoax letter is usually easily spotted. It is invariably written to the length of a letter on the page – in other words cut to a neat 150 words or so. It is often written in a childish hand and purports to be from a teacher. One letter I got read: 'Dear Virginia, I have a problem. I am a gym mistress and a lesbian. I have no friends. I am covered in spots and sores. I have venereal disease and I don't know how I got it because I have never had a boyfriend. I am very lonely because everyone hates me and to make things worse I have smelly armpits.'

Smelling more a rat than an armpit, I sent off my standard statted letter which says: 'Dear Reader, Sometimes we have to reassure ourselves that someone has actually sent a letter. Will you please write back to confirm that you indeed did send me a letter that you wished to be answered?' Two days later the phone rang and a furious voice boomed: 'I have never sent you a letter in my life!' It was the gym mistress. 'It must be one of my pupils. Will you please send it back to me so that I can bring the culprit to justice!'

To send a hoax like that must be one of the cruellest ways of getting back at anyone. Imagine scampering downstairs in the morning to see a letter on the mat. 'Oooh goody!' you squeal, glad that at last someone has sent you something other than a bill or an offer to you, the Tronside family, to win a million pounds. You open it up and read: 'Dear Virginia, I am so sorry to hear you are covered with suppurating sores, you have no friends, you worry about your personal freshness and you are a lesbian....' Make your day, wouldn't it?

The Motherly Woman shook her head in horror at the idea that people could be so cruel. 'And men, do they ever write to you?'

At *Woman* I only got a few letters from men. Of course it was hardly likely they would write to *Woman*, considering the title of the magazine, but although for a while I had a spot on the page called 'The Other Half', specially for men, I often had a job filling it. Barely fifty-two men actually wrote in each *year*. And if they did, the questions were invariably about sex.

It was surprising the number of women who expressed astonishment that more men didn't write in. But *Woman* is, after all, a women's magazine. And if I had a problem I wouldn't write in to *Auto-Trader* or *Pumping Iron Monthly*. And there just aren't similar magazines for men except individual hobby magazines or style magazines like *Arena* – and these don't carry problem pages. Why don't they? I guess it's because men don't want them. If these magazines felt that having a problem page would be a popular feature which would sell copies, they'd have one. And quite honestly, I sometimes wonder why, when I discussed it with some women, they felt it was so sad and tragic that men didn't write in. In a pitying and patronizing kind of way they'd say, 'Ah, it's because men have not learned to express their feelings.'

Why should they express their feelings? Recognizing and expressing your feelings is a way of coping that most women find extremely useful – certainly I do myself – but why anyone else should go along with this is a mystery. It is not a moral virtue to recognize and express feelings – it's simply a way of dealing with problems that some people find extremely useful. *But some don't.* There are other ways of dealing with problems, one of which is to suppress them.

And it does seem as if men do quite often manage to suppress their problems successfully with the result that after a matter of a short time, the problem has gone away or resolved itself. Having said all this, the idea that men don't express their feelings or write in for help was completely disproved when I arrived at the *Sunday Mirror* where at least half the letters I get are from men.

Their main worries are sex, bereavement, loneliness and divorce. I get a lot of letters from lonely men who've never had a girlfriend, who are chronically shy and feel they will be single and unloved for the rest of their lives.

'All I want is someone to love, someone to share my life with, someone to have a family with. Does this have to be denied to me?' is a common plea. Other men write in worrying about being gay or transvestite, and many's the man with problems about access to his children.

Otherwise I have letters from anyone you can think of. I've had letters from head teachers and children, health workers and prostitutes, doctors and prisoners, black and white, letters from wealthy people and broke people and letters from all over the world.

Irma Kurtz says her American letters are very different from the ones she gets from English readers. 'They are much much more over the top,' she says. 'They must read Mills and Boon. They write things like "He is the only man for me ... bells rang when we kissed" and what I get a lot of is "I'm 23 years old, I have four children, my last two marriages have not worked out, now where can I find another man?" The only thing you can say is: "Don't, for God's sake, don't get another man!" '

The letters come on paper with embossed addresses, letters written on the backs of envelopes, letters written on office invoice slips or, saddest of all, they come depressed and suicidal on paper that has a cheery Snoopy at the top. Sometimes you can just tell what kind of people they are by their writing. There are neat men whose writing slopes dangerously backwards; teenagers who do circles on top of their 'i's and sign their often extremely depressed letters by drawing a smiling face inside one of the loops of their name. There are crazy letters in green ink from crazy people; there are shaky letters from the elderly and there are dreadful wonky letters in unformed writing from people I always hope have not put their address at the top. Irma Kurtz, in her book *Sob Sister* (Michael Joseph, 1981) gives a graphic description of how the agony aunt heroine feels when opening a sack of letters from the magazine she works for:

> When Della slit the flap of the big envelope, the enclosed letters spilled out, expanding to a strength that seemed too great for the space that had contained them. Envelopes, hundreds of them, lay before her in pastels, some white, many cheap brown. There were glimpses of handwriting Della understood without reading the words; the tiny hand of an introvert, an anorexic's elaborate script, the underlined stabbings of schizophrenia, a liar's scrawl, the childish loops of repression. They clamoured like voices, they wept, they whined, they called out to Della. It was like a torrent of runny noses.

And that says it all. Very rarely do I get anything out of the norm. Only very occasionally do I get a lovely card or letter from someone who is really grateful for the advice she's been given and tells in detail of what a recovery she's made. But generally, people don't write back. Perhaps it's because so much of my work is to do with referring people on to other organizations; perhaps it's because the advice works or the situation has changed or that the advice has simply shed a useful side-light on an issue which has helped the reader come to her own conclusions. But one reason I think they don't reply is (at least, I hope it is) that it's rather like going to a doctor. If he gives you antibiotics for flu, you don't speed back, two weeks later, to tell him how marvellously they worked. You wait till the next time – and often I do get letters from people saying: 'You won't remember me, but I wrote three years ago with a problem and you gave such marvellous advice ... and now I'm writing to you with a different problem....'

What *kind* of people write in? When I arrived at *Woman* I won't deny that I was expecting letters from a load of wallies who couldn't manage their own lives. How wrong I was. From day one I've not stopped admiring and often feeling humbled by the people who write in to me. I know that sounds dreadfully sentimental, but it's true. They are almost without exception intelligent, articulate and often extremely sensitive, private people. They often have a very good grasp of the situation – and are frequently so sensitive that they believe that the whole situation is their fault even when it clearly isn't.

Those who write in to agony columns are, of course, a self-selecting group. It is a rare person who's sufficiently motivated to seek help for a problem outside the normal social framework of friends, relatives and doctors; an even rarer person who will take the trouble to write down everything surrounding the problem to a complete stranger hoping for an objective assessment. They're brave – because they know that as doctors can easily put them down face to face, so it would be even easier for me to put them down in a letter. Sometimes they beg for a particular answer: 'Please tell me I'm not wrong to leave my husband who has put me in hospital every two months with his beatings,' or 'Please tell me I'm just being utterly stupid and I have to pull myself together and put up with my husband's infidelity.' They often look to me as a kind of social litmus paper. 'My husband says that all women put up with their husbands going out to the pub every night and having anal sex whenever their husbands feel like it. Is this really true?'

All the letters that come in are treated confidentially. That is, no one reads them except me and my dwindling staff. Letters that have lived in the locked filing cabinet are shredded after nine months. And I do get quite a lot of anonymous letters – which is infuriating when you know you could help the person who wrote. 'My husband opens all my mail so I can't give my address' is a common excuse; or sometimes the writer can't give an address because, even at eighteen, their parents still open their post! Sometimes a wife and her husband open each other's post, taking sharing everything a great deal too far. Sometimes they get frightened that the postman might read my reply or that it might get delivered to the wrong address – or they believe that I print everything that comes in within a few days so it'll be guaranteed an immediate answer on the page. Sadly, at *Woman*, by the time I could put an answer on the page if I felt it was desperately urgent, it was almost certainly far, far too late to do anything about it because of our late printing dates. At the *Sunday Mirror* it takes two weeks, but even so it often isn't editorially right to put a particular letter on the page – perhaps I've mentioned such a problem too recently – so the letter has to wait.

Not all letters are odd, anonymous, dramatic or bizarre, however. Indeed, most are on everyday topics that nearly everyone can identify with, even if they haven't experienced them. They are all from people who are, for one reason or another, in pain.

*   *   *   *

The Neighbour's Partner passes by with a large greasy plate, totally empty except for a pile of cocktail sticks. 'The baby's back,' he says, 'if you want to see him.'

'No, no,' says the Motherly Woman. 'She's just about to tell me all about the subjects people write in about. Aren't you?'

'Well, it's rather difficult....'

'Surely not. There can't be more than ten basic problems, surely?'

'There Can't Be More Than Ten Basic Problems ..?'

When Marje takes on a new letter-writer she always asks one question. She takes them to a pile of letters and asks them what they see. They usually look baffled and say: 'A pile of letters' but Marje shakes her head. The applicant might now hazard: 'A pile of problems.' Not the right answer. Finally the poor applicant is told, kindly, that it is not a pile of letters or a pile of problems, it is a pile of letters from *people* with problems.

And that's how I see that pile, too. Which is why it is always so difficult to answer questions like 'What kinds of problems do you get?' Because I, and other agony aunts, see our letters more in terms of 'What kinds of people do you get?'

Of course, various themes run through the letters, but each letter is usually a combination of problems and, like fingerprints, none are exactly like any other. In Irma Kurtz's book, *Sob Sister*, the agony aunt heroine has got her problems taped.

Under Della's desk there were eight plastic bags designed, originally, to contain builders' tools. They were labelled: 'Orgasms', 'Pregnancy: wanted and unwanted', 'Tits, noses, superfluous hair', 'Weight: over and under', 'Infidelity', 'Depression and psychosis', 'Sex: homo, trans and bi-' and 'Miscellaneous'.

43

But in real life the problems can't be neatly sorted into order. The letters are more like a crowd of people, each with its own personality. The recurring themes that run through them are like coloured threads, so that at the end of each letter the writer has written of so many different problems and with such different emphasis on each that he has woven himself a distinctive textile, a completely original personality print, which is his and his alone.

However, whenever anyone asks me what problems I get asked about most often, my answer is invariably: 'Loneliness and depression because people aren't married, or loneliness and depression because they are.' It's a glib answer – to rather a glib question. It's a question that's as difficult to answer as the one that goes: 'Have the problems changed over the years?' I feel I'm too close to them. It's rather like asking the ambulance man, in the middle of giving the kiss of life, whether accidents have changed over the years. Saving lives is saving lives and that's all, really, that concerns him. When you are on a battlefield tending the wounded, you don't look at the experience objectively, with a view to doing a anthropological survey of war in this day and age. You just get down to business.

There's also often an assumption that as topics become fashionable in the more trendy papers like the *Guardian*, these fashions are reflected in the letters to the problem pages in the more downmarket papers. But it's very rarely I'm asked questions about whether a mother should go out to work or stay at home to look after her children, whether she should keep her single name even though she's married, whether it would be wise to let a son take a year off before university, whether vitamins are good for children's intelligence. This is the stuff of feature pages. The stuff of the problem pages is simply misery.

Broadly, the major themes are depression, loneliness, lack of confidence, marriage problems, panic attacks, bereavement, phobias, health problems, teenage anxieties, children, and, of course, sex. And then there are a whole variety of other problems that pop up on a regular basis – blushing, adoption (and how to trace natural parents), acne, age (and caring for elderly relatives), how you can choose a baby's sex (you can't), cosmetic surgery, incest, rape, battered wives, debt, drinking problems and post-natal depression. One of the most touching letters I had was from a woman, presumably suffering from post-natal depression, who tearfully wrote to me upset that her six-month-old baby (or rather, the father, on the baby's behalf) had not sent her a Mother's Day card!

People write to me with problems about pets – jealous pets or dying pets – Asian girls write when they come up against conflicts of cultures, and I get masses of letters on eating problems like anorexia and bulimia, homosexuality, shoplifting, gambling, insomnia, menopause and HRT, smoking, snoring, tranquillizer addiction and infertility. I'm often sent chain letters to destroy – rather touchingly readers even send me the original chain letter photocopied twenty times – and there's a constant flow of queries about headaches, nits, hypnosis, irritable bowel syndrome, jealousy, missing people, problem neighbours, sweating and personal freshness, mothers-in-law and pre-menstrual syndrome. And many, many others.

But one of the biggest problems by far is loneliness. The following letter is typical of the hundreds I get on exactly the same sort of lines.

I hope you can help me out. My name is Alan and I am 30 years old. I weigh fifteen stone and have receding hair. I know I am overweight and seem unattractive to the opposite sex. I have considered dieting and I am sure I could achieve this if I had a lady in my life. I am very shy and I know you won't believe this but I am still a virgin and have never had a sexual relationship with a lady. I have kissed a few and been out on a very few dates. But I am very lonely and really need someone to love as I feel I have so much love to give someone. I have spent a few years looking after my mum and that has stopped me doing things. But now I think time is running out for me and I don't look forward to much nowadays. I really would like to make the effort and have considered clubs. But my weight and shyness prevent me doing so. Please, please could you help me find a lady to love and spend some time with because I need someone and I am sure there is someone out there in the same situation.

I have a leaflet on *Loneliness* which would go out with a sympathetic letter – a leaflet that, yes, does include the corny old suggestions of dating agencies and going to evening classes. I explain, however, that even if you don't meet anyone through a dating agency, just the act of going out and sitting in a crowded place with someone else does wonders for the morale; and that though you're unlikely to find anyone at the evening class, who knows who you might meet on the way to it? Certainly you'll never meet up with that old schoolfriend you lost touch with if you sit at home behind closed doors – but you might meet him or her if you get out on the streets.

Phobias and obsessions account for a large number of letters, too. Some women, particularly, suffer from a fear of dying, of being sick, or even of eating in public.

One woman had such a fear of spiders that when she saw one behind the hot tap she was transfixed for half an hour (with the hot tap running) until she got the courage to rush out of the house and enlist the help of some workmen over the road who came and removed it for her. It was two hours before she could bear to go back.

Agoraphobia is a very common problem as well – and usually those who write in are in a Catch 22 position, where they know help is available but can't, because of their illness, go out to get it. Many women are agoraphobic because they fear they may have a panic attack when they're out. Panic attacks are terrible feelings of faintness, breathlessness and general about-to-die feelings, accompanied (not surprisingly) by a racing heart and total panic. Whenever I write about panic attacks I get a very big response.

Obsessions are almost as common as phobias. Many is the woman who has a cleaning obsession – to the point, occasionally, where she cannot touch her children when they come home from school for fear of being contaminated by germs. And I had a sad letter from a boy obsessed with his face. He believed it was like plasticine, that whenever he touched it it would go out of shape. He also believed that when he ate, his bones would click out of place and his face would look uneven. He was so upset by what he thought was his terrible appearance, that he went out in a crash helmet – even to the shops. The result was that people looked at him, thus confirming his fears that he did, indeed, look very odd. The saddest thing was that he sent me photos of himself and he was an extremely good-looking young man.

Mothers-in-law are another common problem. Most people may think they're a joke – but the people who write in to me don't.

One woman had a mother-in-law who visited three times a day and stayed for an hour each time, tapping on the windows, or waiting on the doorstep when she was out. When the daughter-in-law dropped a tactful hint that she felt pressured by having so many visitors, her mother-in-law settled down for a nice cup of tea and sympathized, saying how she couldn't bear it when people popped in all the time, either.

Another woman complained that she was considering divorce because on Mother's Day she had found, in her husband's pocket, a card to his mum with the words 'To the only woman I have ever loved' written inside. In vain did her husband try to convince her that this was simply a message written to buck his old mum up.

I get an awful lot of letters from young people. (How I hate that phrase – it sounds so patronizing and I remember cringing when adults used to say how much they 'loved young people' when I was young. Still, I'm afraid I've now got to the age where I, too, 'love young people', which is perhaps why they write to me.) They write pages and pages about boys they have sometimes never even spoken to, convinced they have found love at last. Every sighting is noted and described in great detail – how he half-smiled, or how she felt him looking at her, or how their eyes met, or how she's convinced he's too shy to say hello – the letter usually ending with the words 'Do you think he's as in love with me as I am with him?'

Teenagers write about crushes they have on their teachers, on their friends, and about the shameful fact that they are still virgins at sixteen. They ask me how to kiss and how to get a girlfriend.

They write, too, obsessed by their looks. Their boobs are too big, or too small; their legs are a funny shape; their teeth stick out; their noses are awful; they have far too much hair above the bikini line; they are much too fat; they are much too thin.

These are tricky ones to reply to. To tell them that it is themselves that matter, not their noses, which is true, is all the same an awful slap in the face to a teenager who lacks confidence and pins it all on his or her appearance. I do write back pointing out that people like Barbra Streisand are very attractive, nose and all, but really a teenager needs more than that, and these letters have to be particularly long and confidence-boosting.

Perhaps depression is the biggest problem of all, though the people who write in often don't realize its depression they're suffering from. They give a list of textbook symptoms – they wake up early, they feel better as the day goes on, they feel physically tired, they can't stop crying, they feel worthless and unloved – but it never occurs to them they are suffering from depression. As one who suffered from depression for years I know how agonizing it can be. I remember being unable even to feel anything at all; I remember crying and crying endlessly while not feeling anything, and telling my family that I wasn't feeling unhappy, I was just crying and that what was so awful was that I couldn't feel anything, not even unhappiness. It was like being in an emotional prison. I remember being unable to feel hunger or tiredness – and the only thing I could feel was either a terrible physical lethargy, as if my body was filled with poisoned lead, or the most excruciating physical torture of tension, as if someone had caught up every sinew in my body and was slowly tightening them all up by winding them round a stick. My leaflet on depression is, as you can imagine, one of my longest, and I recommend every trick in the book to overcome depression. But obviously the first step is the doctor, even though many people seem to prefer to feel suicidal than consider taking 'tablets'.

They often write to me saying, 'I can't see my doctor because he'll only prescribe pills', which a) isn't true. He'll probably prescribe medication *and* a visit to a behavioural psychologist – and he should look at your real-life problems as well, like housing and so on. And b) medication can work miracles for people. Depression is often a result of some kind of chemical imbalance and there's no question that suicidal people have returned to their bouncing selves after a course of anti-depressants. But, as I say, the trend these days is to combine medication with some kind of therapy because it's found that people tend to get much better much more quickly that way.

To show you the sort of letters I so often get on depression, I'm quoting a letter from a twenty-year-old man in full – and I'm sure you can see how annoying it for us agony aunts to have to cut letters like this down to a single paragraph. It's impossible to do it and still retain the poignant flavour:

I'm now twenty and have been very depressed for the last three years. At the start of this depression, although I was miserable and unhappy all the time, I kept telling myself that I would get over this depression and would emerge as a much stronger and better person. However, three years on I feel my life is at an end. All I do is cry and feel suicidal all the time. In actual fact the only thought that is on my mind is what the best way of killing myself is. I don't believe I can get any worse. I've now even wrote a suicide note and dated it the date of my twenty-first birthday as I honestly believe that if things don't start to improve I will take my life on that day. Family and friends don't understand and accuse me of self-pity. I cannot win. If I put a brave face on they claim I'm faking depression and there is nothing wrong with me, whereas when I show them I'm really low they say I should stop sitting around and go and get a job. I feel under constant pressure and criticism all the time at home. I know that it is my low self-esteem that makes me feel set upon by family and friends but they don't understand that this pressure makes me feel worse. Even when I try to talk rationally to my parents, we always end up shouting with me in tears. So nowadays I say nothing and just suffer in silence. But having nobody to talk to makes me feel very lonely and isolated. So as a result this loneliness makes me even more depressed and at the end of every day I go upstairs and cry myself to sleep.

I've really tried to help myself by tackling my fears and causes of my depression. I've seen a few counsellors and family counsellors both on the NHS and private, but they don't seem to have helped. They get angry with me for not fully helping myself and I get angry at myself and frustrated for not showing any improvement and because I feel extremely miserable and suicidal all the time. I suppose I know deep down I'm not helping myself a hundred per cent but I honestly can't motivate myself to help myself. I've done that for the first two years of my depression. Endured all that excess pain and misery and feel I've nothing to show for it.

So now for the last year I've given in and accepted defeat. I feel so emotionally and physically tired. Now I can't seem to be able to do anything apart from sleep, breathe and cry (the only emotion I feel that reminds me that I'm still living). I think that's why I'm writing to you, Virginia. I know you yourself said you suffered years of depression so you know how I must feel. I don't want you to say hang on in there, give it time. I want you, well, not to say, but understand that if I do take my life that you will be thinking: 'It's okay John, you're free now, no more pain and misery. You can rest now.'

I mean is it so wrong to want to die? I see it as not all of us were born to live long happy lives and I'm sure death will be heaven to the way I feel.

PS I hope this letter doesn't make you feel a little responsible for my actions as I would be angry if you did. I know you understand and all the best.

What has happened to this boy that he's getting no help with his problem? He hasn't mentioned whether he's seen a psychiatrist or whether he's been on anti-depressants. How can I construct an answer that will make this boy feel as if someone really understands what he's going through and convince him that it really *is* worth hanging on, at least till a few years after his twenty-first birthday? Perhaps the saddest part of that letter is his great sensitivity and sense of punishing responsibility – he even begs a stranger like me not to feel responsible if he kills himself. I will write back to him – and probably follow the letter up with another letter. But more likely than not I will never hear from him again. I will never know if my letter helped or if he got better of his own accord or whether he did indeed commit suicide. His letter to me is rather like a letter sent up the chimney to Father Christmas; but my letter back goes hurtling, as far as I'm concerned, into a kind of outer space as well. I presume he gets my reply but I may never know.

Divorce is another source of problems – particularly access to children. New partners are jealous of old partners, new partners are jealous of old children, too. Step-families can be minefields of misery, with neither set of children getting on with their new 'parent' or their new siblings. Parents write in desperation when they find they only have access to their children once a fortnight; other parents write in asking whether it's true they have to let their partner see their children every weekend because the night before he comes they scream and cry with fear and misery.

And a typical problem of the step-family came from a new stepdad who had arrived in a family of three boys whose father only saw them once a year, if that. The eldest called him Dave, the middle one called him Uncle Dave and the youngest called him Dad. But 'friends' had been saying that they should all call him Dad. What should he do? Of course I wrote telling him to leave things as they were – and perhaps to point out to the youngest that though he was welcome to call him Dad he must remember he had another, real, Dad, as well.

Another stepfather was so angry that his stepdaughter didn't call him Dad that she had started to wet the bed. This resulted in the family insisting that visits from the real father, whom she loved dearly, were cut down. What a mess.

Children always seem to get a raw deal. And I'm constantly amazed by the number of letters I get from women who mention, briefly, that they have three children under the age of ten, say, and then continue to outline plans for leaving the marriage for their lover. No word about the children ever appears in the letter again. Since I think that children are the most important people in the whole world, I'm baffled by the attitude that so many people seem to have towards their own kids. I regard bringing up children as the most rewarding (and, true, therefore the most frustrating and challenging) job in the world.

Perhaps the problem is that so many people seem to find it hard to understand children, even though they have all been children themselves once. We're constantly being told that children are people and therefore should be treated with respect. But while this is true, children, though people, are not adults.

As you wouldn't expect a six-month-old child to walk, nor should you expect a teenager to have much concept of mortality, for instance. That's why teenagers often experiment with drugs and start smoking despite the known dangers. They can't understand that one day they might die. Similarly, though you can expect a five-year-old to *say* 'Thank you', you can't expect him to feel gratitude – particularly to his parents for what they do. It's a feeling that just hasn't been developed at that age.

An American feminist recently summed up my view well when she said: 'A child is a temporarily disabled and stunted version of a larger person whom you will someday know. Your job is to help them overcome the disabilities associated with their size and inexperience so that they get on with being that larger person.'

Love your child to distraction, I say, but never forget that it needs examples to look up to. If you don't want your child to lie, don't lie yourself. If you want your child to say sorry when he's done wrong, say sorry in similar circumstances yourself. If you want your child not to be violent, don't hit him yourself. If you want your child to say 'thank you' to you, you must say 'thank you' to him now and again.

Americans 'raise' their children. We 'bring them up' – but all too often haul them up or squash them down instead. I like the idea of 'raising'. It reminds me of seeds, needing nothing but water, air, food, lots of attention, pest-control to stop them being damaged by outside forces and the odd trellis to lean against when they get wobbly.

So many people who write to me seem not to understand their children's needs. They write in despair saying their children are 'uncontrollable' or that their babies cry all the time and that the health visitor has suggested ignoring them because they 'just want attention'. I never understand this line. It's like saying that you shouldn't offer a meal to a starving child because he 'just wants food'.

Then there are the interfering mums who seem to spend their time at home reading their teenage daughters' diaries – and being horrified when they see what flies out of Pandora's Box. And there are the parents who insist on reading their children's post even when they are seventeen and eighteen, and won't let them stay out beyond ten o'clock at night.

All of these letters are difficult enough to reply to, but worst are what I call the 'impossible' letters. They run along the lines of:

> I'm living on my own but my ex-husband comes round and I sleep with him sometimes. I'm also going out with two boyfriends who my husband knows about. I'm *in love* with Pete who works in Loughborough. He's asked me to sleep with him but I haven't yet. And there's Tim, who lives nearby and who I love dearly but am not in love with. (I'm in love with my ex-husband, too, by the way.) Pete lives with his mother and is a bit of a workaholic and wants neither marriage nor children; he says he has no other girlfriend. But I'm not sure if Tim doesn't really want to marry a younger woman so he can have children. He has never said he loves me but says actions speak louder than words. He doesn't have another girlfriend. My husband says he can't guarantee he will never come back but I'm still hoping.
>
> Should I a) get a divorce b) sleep with Tim c) spend more time with Pete and/or sleep with him?

Er....

The other impossible questions are what psychologist Eric Berne called the 'Yes, but ...' problems. They go:

> 'Dear Virginia, I am married to a violent man but I love him very much. I am also agoraphobic. Don't tell me to go to a Woman's Aid refuge because I love my husband so much I don't want to leave him. But how can I stop him hitting me? And don't tell me to see my doctor about the agoraphobia because I won't go. I've read lots of books on the subject but none help me. Don't suggest tapes because they're useless. But how can I get out and about again?'

What on earth can one say to her?

Marriage problems are now called 'partnership' problems or 'relationship' problems. But it doesn't matter what name you give them. They abound. As my grandmother wryly pointed out to my mother as they sat in the register office waiting for my mother to get married: 'Marriage is like a besieged fortress. Those inside would do anything to get out; those outside would do anything to get in.'

Generally I only hear about the problems, but there's a general buzz from the other letters I get that tells me that there are enormously large numbers of incredibly happy relationships out there. People write in with problems but often they add that their wives or husbands have been marvellously supportive; certainly the many letters I get from bereaved people paint a picture of a married life that often seems entirely unclouded and truly blessed.

Communication does seem to be the biggest problem in any marriage and until a couple realize that the only way to clear the air or sort anything out is to sit down and talk about it, any problem usually remains – unless it goes away of its own accord. Dropped hints don't work; and it's sad to hear of how many couples clearly do not really know how each other ticks. I'm not saying that the vast majority of couples don't have relationships that are slightly marred by some hidden resentment on either side – and, God knows, we all know how difficult it is to sit down with those closest to us and actually broach some dreadfully uncomfortable subject that neither person really wants to talk about – but when these resentments and grudges become relationship-threatening there's really no way out other than facing up to them and discussing them.

The letter I had that summed up communication problems best of all came from a woman who, looking for reassurance of her husband's true love, suggested to him that they had an open marriage 'not because I really wanted one but because I'd like to hear him say "Certainly not!" But now I find he's slept with his secretary three times. He said he would never have done it if I hadn't seemed so keen on the idea and nagged him into it. He says it was only physical, that she was a dreadful girl and he only strung her along. This made me feel worse because he must be so callous to behave like that to her.'

The other perennial problem in a marriage is a partner (usually male) who won't help around the house at all. He comes back from work with a four-pack, turns on the telly, eats his tea, refuses to wash up, won't help with the children, and slumps into bed often, it seems, wearing his underclothes which he never washes till they come off on Saturday night for sex. These lumpish chauvinists only come alive when they are putting their foot down about any independence for their wives, and when begged, become abusive and violent. Like WC Fields, when asked by a feminist whether he believed in clubs for women, they would reply: 'Only when all else fails.'

Other problems come from wives who work just as hard as their husbands in jobs – and still have to come back to all the housework and washing and so on.

Jealousy's another familiar problem. Women often write to me because their husbands, although apparently loving, loyal men, cannot stop their eyes roving when they're out. Or the wives or girlfriends catch them reading pornographic magazines or watching blue videos. It's difficult for some men to realize how what they see as a harmless turn-on can be so upsetting to their partners.

Often a partner's jealousy is founded. A roving husband will have an affair, be caught out and sheepishly return to his wife, usually claiming he loves her to distraction and will never do it again. What so often happens, though, is that, as far as he is concerned, that is that – while the wife is tormented by thoughts of what went on and longs to discuss it. But while a discussion would help her to get it all out of her system and lay it all to rest, the man sees a discussion as raking up the past and keeping it alive. But the wife, unless they do talk it out, can carry on the resentment and unhappiness for years. I had a letter once from an eighty-year-old woman who had never felt happy again after her husband had had an affair, just like the one I've described, in his forties. It was constantly on her mind. He refused to speak about it. But had they hammered it out, the ghost could have been laid to rest long ago and she could have got on with living her life.

Jealousy of a different sort comes usually from men, some of whom seem to insist their partners stay at home all the time when they are at work, ringing them up constantly to check they are not out having affairs. The poor women are only allowed to shop in the company of their husband, might perhaps be allowed out on their own to take the children to school and collect them, and are under a barrage of constant accusations. A car only has to pass the door more than once and the man will become convinced that it is his wife's lover, cruising by trying to catch a glimpse of her. These wretchedly sad, insecure men frequently turn into threatened, violent monsters when their unfounded suspicions get the better of them.

Finally, there are the problems with married men. Women are always writing in to me with pitiful accounts of their affairs with married men. Sometimes (but hardly ever) the man leaves his wife and marries his mistress. Then the new wife writes to me astonished when this philanderer goes and does exactly the same thing to her and runs off with someone else.

Women involved with married men will, it seems to me, believe anything. One woman told me that the married man she was having an affair with had assured her that he wasn't having sex with his wife, though they still slept in a double bed and the wife was now pregnant. He claimed it was the result of a drunken one-off which was a complete accident. I wrote back saying that if this woman really believed he wasn't having regular sex with his wife then perhaps she believed the moon was blue cheese, crusts made her hair curl and that if she held her breath accidentally when she was asleep she'd die.

When asked what present a mistress could buy her married lover for Christmas (not after-shave, obviously, or jewellery, but something personal) I replied that the best present she could give him was the boot. That would be a very personal present which would enable him to get on in peace and, hopefully, harmony, with his family and children.

People write saying that 'we both resisted it, both being married, but in the end it was too powerful for us and, like magnets, we were drawn together'. Such letters make me terribly fed up. 'It' was too powerful? What was? Isn't it a case of them being too weak? And what's all this about being like magnets? They're people, for God's sake, with free will!

As you can gather, my sympathies are not with people who have affairs with married men – probably stemming from knowing what it felt like as a child to have a mum who had affairs while she was married. I know what dreadful damage they did to my parents' marriage and, by extension, to me.

The only way to break the spell of a married man, if anyone's so foolish as to get involved with one, is to meet the wife. Many is the letter I've had on the lines of: 'We met and discussed personal, intimate aspects of our private lives and learnt the truth about him. His life has been built on a tissue of lies and deceit. He's often made his wife out to be a cruel and unpleasant woman, but she's simply a woman and a mother.'

The one topic I haven't touched on, however, is probably the culprit in all these affairs in the first place. Perhaps it deserves a special mention because I get so many letters on the subject. What is it? What do you think? Sex, of course.

*   *   *   *

'SEX?' Suddenly the Blazer is back, scooting to a halt like Bugs Bunny after a carrot. 'Did you say sex?' He is followed by a friend who works in Computer Programming. 'I said I'd come back and I have. And we seem to have returned at the right time, haven't we?'

Behind him more people are cramming into the room. I can hear the baby howling in a corner and can see the bouncing head of my neighbour who is obviously trying to rock him into peace. A glugging sound in my paper cup tells me that the Blazer is topping me up once more. 'Look, I must go and see that baby,' I say apologetically. 'I only came to give him a present.'

'And so you shall,' says the Blazer, steering me to a chair and sitting me down. I am surrounded by people's knees, thoroughly trapped. 'We want to hear all about your sexy letters.'

'On one condition,' I say. 'I'm starving. I suppose,' I add wistfully, 'there aren't any of those delicious sausages left, are there?'

At the word 'sausages' the Blazer explodes with laughter. 'Sausages' seems to be a word that sets some men off like kids at school whispering 'knickers' in the dorm.

'It's all been very interesting,' says the Motherly Woman, 'but I think I will go and get some orange squash. I think some people could do with a few soft drinks.' She leaves for the kitchen.

While the Blazer is sausage-bound, the Computer Programmer smiles rather shyly. 'I bet you get some pretty filthy stuff, don't you?' he says, encouragingly.

'I do,' I say. 'And some pretty sad stuff as well.'

'Some Pretty Filthy Stuff ...'

'Dear Vagina, I have a problem with my virginia.' Thus started one of my many letters on the topic of sex.

However shy an agony aunt you are – and shy I certainly was when I arrived at *Woman* – a letter like that is somewhat of an ice-breaker. That's a letter that has to be shared with someone, and before you know where you are you and the rest of your staff are all screaming with laughter and the word vagina – a word that is not a much-used part of my vocabulary – is being bandied around like nobody's business.

When I arrived at *Woman*, despite being a child of the 'sixties' – which is enough to make you know more about sex than any one in their right minds would ever ask – I was even more embarrassed about talking about it than I am today. And even now, though I can quite happily write words like 'penis' or 'testicles' or 'clitoris', I'm still not entirely happy saying them. If I do (and I can say them quite loudly, with a confident smile, too) there's still a tiny person inside me with her hands over her ears saying: 'Virginia! How *could* you!'

And I was relieved to find out that when Peggy Makins first came to *Woman* as Evelyn Home, she thought that 'fucking' meant 'very' – as in 'fucking fine day, innit?'

Still, I had to overcome my embarrassment just to deal with the everyday problems at *Woman*. I'll never forget one of my more elderly letter-writers coming into my office one day with a letter in her hand saying: 'Virginia – this woman wants to know what a –' and she consulted the piece of paper

61

– "flow-job" is. Or *is* it "flow-job?" ' She handed me the letter.

'Blow-job,' I said, cunningly using a combination of a fluent, understanding smile culled from watching people like Philip Hodson closely on the telly, and a deep, confident, compassionate Thatcher-like whisper. I handed it back.

She looked completely blank. 'But Virginia, what exactly *is* a blow-job?' she asked.

I hesitated. 'Um,' I said. 'Er. Well, it's when a man puts his, ah, um in a woman's, er, mouth and she kinds of sucks, kind of you know, oral sex,' I finished hastily.

The letter-answerer looked increasingly amazed. 'But if it involves sucking, why is it called a blow-job?' she asked.

I snatched the letter from her. 'I'll answer it myself,' I said.

It's so easy to write, so difficult to say. But to be quite honest I still don't have the answer to her question. Why *is* it called a blow-job? Why, indeed, is it called a job at all? Although it's quite a cheery thing to do for someone, the word 'job' smacks rather too much to me of those awful sexual 'tasks' that sex therapists always seem to be setting their clients. Books on sex are full of horrible 'tasks' and 'homework', all of which seem to involve stripping off with a straight face and examining yourself in front of a mirror with lubricating jelly. I mean!

As you will have gathered by now, like most people who appear to talk quite easily about sex on the page, I'm just as hung-up as the next person. Which I think is fine, because most of the people who write to me are like that, too. And if I were some kind of three-in-a-bed-and-if-all-three-of-you-don't-have-simultaneous-orgasms-there's-something-wrong-with-you type of person, I don't think they'd get much comfort writing to me. If you write to me asking if tying each other up and licking peanut butter off each other is normal I'm not going to answer, 'Anything that gives pleasure to both partners is normal.' I'm going to reply: 'There's nothing wrong with what you're doing, it can do you no harm, I'm really glad you both enjoy it and keep at it as long as you like. But as for normal – no. Rather unusual.'

Irma Kurtz discourages questions about sex altogether. 'They'd love to write to me about sex but they've discovered that I don't like it,' she says. 'It's not that I don't like sex but I just don't like other people's sex lives. I'm not interested in how other people carry on in bed. To tell people what to do with honey and high-heeled shoes is just tacky.'

I don't get many honey and high-heeled shoes letters. Most of the letters I get about sex are surprisingly humdrum. But sex deserves a chapter of its own because such a large proportion of the letters that come in to the problem page are about sex, and one of the advantages of a problem page as far as sex goes, over any other kind of help you get for other problems, is that it is far, far easier to write rude than speak rude. Readers can elaborate on all kinds of embarrassing sexual problems on paper which they could never in a hundred years say to anyone's face. It's one thing to write about 'orgasms' and 'coming' and 'semen' and 'masturbation' but another to yammer about them to your friends. Or your acquaintances. Or your doctor, who is, whatever anyone says, often even more embarrassed than you about the subject.

I once attended a Marriage Guidance Council (as it then was) sex workshop (yes, workshop) on a training weekend. A tremendously upper-class white-haired old marriage guidance lady in sandals led a discussion on sex for a variety of trainees, from church counsellors to personnel officers. 'Now, let's be frank and discuss sex!' she boomed. 'I'm going to say a word to each of you and you must all describe it in detail.'

It was a cringe-making session. Luckily I'd already got my glib front up and could talk suavely about 'G-spots', 'vaginal walls', 'lubricating jelly', 'prostate glands', not to mention 'penile thrusting', with ghastly frankness. They had to shut me up. But it was pitiful to witness the poor shy male pastoral counsellor trying to describe 'clitoris' in front of a mixed group of people, when it was clear he hadn't a clue where or what it was (even though he was married); and one woman who was training to be a counsellor and who was called on to describe 'testicles' (and give other names for them) was beside herself when she had to reveal to us all that she had never seen her husband's 'thing' let alone 'things' because they always turned the light out when they made love.

This got rather disapproving looks from the counsellors but I thought, why not? I recently had a letter from someone who complained about his wife being terribly tense and hung-up because she insisted on having the light on all the time when they made love so she could see exactly what he was up to. She didn't trust the dark. And I always thought making love in the dark was the sign of someone repressed and hung-up. Phew!

I felt very sorry for these people because they could have been me a few years previously; they were good-natured and intelligent and kindly — and the fact that they were embarrassed didn't seem to me to be a sign of ridiculous prudery but rather a combination of ignorance and natural modesty. But ignorance and natural modesty are not appropriate when you have to discuss these matters with others who are equally, if not more, embarrassed. And so, when answering letters, I have to put my natural reticence to one side and answer frankly. And it has to be said that one good thing did come out of that session for me. Having thought I was the most embarrassed and screwed-up person in the world when it came to discussing sex, I realized that, compared to the bunch I was with, my name could have been not only Masters but Johnson as well.

As Marje Proops says, 'If, way back in the days when I was working on the *Herald*, I'd had a letter from a woman asking how her man's technique can be improved to ensure her satisfactory orgasms, I'd have fainted dead away on the office floor. Now, questions about orgasms are as commonplace as complaints about mothers-in-law.'

The Computer Programmer is looking as if he is about to faint away himself and perches himself on the edge of my chair. I can feel his embarrassment whizzing through the springs.

Very generally, the sex problems I seem to have these days are ones from people who imagine that everyone else is having an absolutely marvellous time in bed and they're having only an averagely good time. What I think they don't realize is that very few people have a marvellous time in bed all the time. To have what you think is an average sex-life is actually pretty high up in the peaks.

The seventies are a lot to blame for giving people a distorted view of sex. And it's only recently that reality has started to creep in. Men don't always feel sexy. Men often say 'No' as well as women. Women don't always have orgasms (or 'organisms' as some of my readers call them). Most couples make love once or twice a week. Intercourse lasts on average between three and ten minutes. Sex often goes in phases – three months of good sex, a month of bad, three weeks without, a couple of great nights one after another ... and so on.

My aim is always to make sex seem less rather than more important. I do this deliberately. I do it because whenever I read a sex-book that is bursting with drawings of couples in extraordinary positions, that encourages couples to make love spontaneously – in the kitchen, in the bathroom, at three o'clock in the afternoon, upstairs, downstairs, wearing saucy underwear, with vibrators, reading pornography and so on, I always feel like a dreadfully dismal Jane. I put the book down feeling like the most horrible, boring, tedious, unsexy person in the world.

When I read a book that says that more marriages have

sexual problems than don't, that the vast majority of couples favour the missionary position, that a survey shows women (or men) don't rate sex high as an essential in the relationship, then I put the book down feeling like Brigitte Bardot. Compared to these dreary, dull couples I seem a right little raver.

I was amazed to read in a recent book published by Relate the suggestion that making a date for making love together was an original and sexy thing to do. All the books I'd been reading up till then had said it was totally unspontaneous and cold. This latest book – in a completely new and radical statement – actually declared that making love in different rooms in the house can be uncomfortable. I always remember reading one sex-book that said in chapter one that 'early experiences of uncomfortable love-making in the back of a car can lead to sex problems later. It is extremely important to feel relaxed, comfortable and secure while making love.' Then in the next chapter what did they recommend? Making love in the bath! The taps! The water turning chilly! The plug coming out accidentally! The cold slippery sides! The grazed shins! The accidental turning on of the cold shower! No thanks.

Men and women write in with very different problems. As my one-time editor at *Woman*, Jane Reed, always used to say, the men wrote in to *Woman* with only three questions: 'How big, how long and how often?' They preceded most of their queries rather sweetly, with the words: 'I hope you don't mind me, a mere male, writing, but ...' and then went on to ask how big, how long or how often. At the *Sunday Mirror*, however, I get a lot more letters about premature ejaculation, impotence and sexual performance declining with age.

Penis size does seem to be a big problem for some men. Despite the fact that research has been done which shows that penis size really does not matter, men still write to me in agonies about sizes. They measure the things as if for a Savile

Row suit, giving me girth at the top, girth at the bottom, length when erect, length when flaccid, length they think they ought to be, length they've read about in porn mags. I feel like writing back asking if they'd like lapels and turn-ups, sir? The problem for men is that as they wee and shower in groups they tend to be able to get good looks at everyone else's equipment. They also fail to realize that although everyone's a different size in this situation, everyone's much of a muchness when their penises are erect.

Women have been known not to be kind to men who appear to have small penises, however. I've more than one letter from lads working in factories who've been set upon by gangs of women, debagged and then become the butt of the most painfully cruel jokes.

I even had a letter at *Woman* from a group of women who were about to embark on a de-bagging. 'We are five women in a packing factory. A new boy has just joined – he's only 17 – and we all laugh at him and make jokes. He's so shy! Now some of the women want to get together and pounce on him, take his trousers off and give him a tickle for a laugh! What do you think? Would it be harmless fun?' I replied by asking them how they would feel if, as shy seventeen-year-old girls, they were pounced on by five big men, had their knickers taken off and were tickled and laughed at. I hope they got the message.

Men are also extremely insecure about how long they last. I recently had a letter from a man who couldn't sleep at night because he 'only lasted fifteen minutes'. He'd probably been reading one of those insecure-making books I mentioned earlier.

Men always seem to think that if everything about sex isn't perfect, then it's their fault. So if their partners don't seem very happy or don't have orgasms, they see their problem as premature ejaculation, never stopping to consider that the real problem might be a woman who takes an age to get an orgasm, or a woman who feels it is her right to reach orgasm through intercourse alone, what's known as a 'no hands' orgasm. Not, actually, that common.

But premature ejaculation is a persistent source of anxiety to many men. 'The biggest response I ever got was on the *Sun*,' says Claire Rayner. 'It was a great British working man's paper and the one thing you couldn't suggest was that the great British working man couldn't get it up. But I had a lot of letters on the subject of premature ejaculation so I managed to get a tiny letter on the page, no more than a column inch, from a man with trigger trouble. He couldn't last long enough, what could he do? I said it was a common problem shared with many. I promised to send him a leaflet. You know how many requests I got for that leaflet just after that one small mention on the page? Eighteen thousand! I got a letter, too, from a man a year later after getting that leaflet and he said it was wonderful, he could last half an hour now. And I thought if I've done no more than give one couple some pleasure in bed, that's not bad.'

Along with the premature ejaculators, I also get a persistent number of letters from men who are unable to ejaculate. This is a problem that is usually psychological, and is a great curse to those who suffer from it. It can be curable with help, however.

Impotence is high on the list of male sexual problems – a problem that, apart from the normal short periods of impotence that every man gets in his life – is increasingly thought to be due to physical rather than psychological problems. Unfortunately, not everyone's doctor seems to have caught on to this latest thinking and frequently send fifty-year-old men away with mutterings about their 'age', nothing to be done or give younger men tranquillizers, advise them to have a couple of drinks and tell them it's all in the mind. Hopeless advice.

'Absolutely hopeless!' cries the Computer Programmer, in a loud, bitter and angry voice, banging the arm of the chair.

We all look at him rather oddly and he goes silent and blushes.

Older men, who perhaps might expect their sex-life to start winding down (and by older I mean over sixty-five) often write in frantically when they find their sex-life is declining. It often turns out of course, that they are on medication for high blood pressure or something – and that their doctor has failed to mention that impotence might be a side-effect.

While women write in about birth control and safe sex, men, predictably, rarely if ever write in about contraception. But I do remember one man who wanted to get a vasectomy as a birthday present for his wife – '... because,' he wrote, 'I don't want any more children.' Notice the 'I'. Talk about giving your mother roller skates for Christmas!

And it seems that few men have the first clue about what turns a woman on. Infuriated by his somewhat unresponsive wife, one man bought her a special short sexy nightie – which she refused to wear. He then lost his temper and threatened that he would go off and have an affair if she didn't put it on. The poor guy simply didn't realize that his wife probably felt frightfully silly in a sexy nightie, that short nighties are dreadfully cold in winter, new nighties are awfully scratchy and, anyway, maybe she didn't like the look of her knobbly knees. Corny as it may sound, a few sweet words, a cuddle on the sofa in front of the telly and a bunch of flowers would probably have turned her on far quicker. And been a lot cheaper, too.

Just as men don't seem to realize that women are turned on by feelings, cuddles and words, however, so women don't seem to realize that men are turned on much more by visual things – like sexy nighties, pornography and so on.

So many women write to me very upset about their partners reading girlie magazines, and though personally I can't see why men shouldn't look at soft porn if they want, if it upsets their partners they should have the good manners to goggle at it in discreet places. Hiding it, by the way, does not mean putting it under the bed, because there it's always discovered. The problem of discovery is compounded by the woman realizing her partner imagines she never cleans under the bed as well, adding insult to injury.

When I got letters from women saying they were upset by men having pin-ups on the office walls, I used to suggest they put up male nudes and see how the men liked that. Looking back, it was a mad idea. I don't think men would mind at all. Men understand being turned on by pictures. Women don't. So if women find pin-ups on the wall upsetting, then it's no big deal for men to keep them in their desk drawers.

One man wrote to me saying he'd just seen some blue films and was keen for his wife to try oral sex with him but she refused. 'I don't understand why a woman in a pornographic movie will do this with a man she's not known for long, while my wife of eight years refuses,' he wrote. I pointed out that everyone's different, and that the fact the actress was paid might have had some bearing on the matter.

I get fetishists writing in with obsessions with high-heeled shoes, rubber sheets and seamed stockings. (The only theory that's come up about these fetishes is that they could be associated with babyhood – that a baby feels rubber sheeting under his bottom, that as he's small, his usual line of vision takes in only his mother's feet and ankles. I wonder whether, if this is true, fetishes will change over the years and the fetishists of the future will be after trainers and tracksuit bottoms, and plastic rather than rubber.)

One wrote in to *Woman* saying: 'I'm mad on stiletto-heeled shoes you used to see girls wearing in the fifties. I get a great turn-on at the sight, touch and sound of them. It may sound silly to you, but I love them and can't bear to hear of anyone throwing them away. I've got a collection of five pairs. My current girlfriend, however, has told me to send them to a jumble sale or burn them; but the thought distresses me so much that I can't. I don't dress up in the shoes or ask my girlfriend to wear them, and my sex life is perfectly normal. I just like them around. What shall I do?' My advice to him was to keep the shoes and send the girlfriend to the jumble sale.

And many men write in anxious about being homosexual.

'My mother has come to terms with the fact that I'm gay, even asking to see photographs of my lover and saying he "looks nice"! The problem is she has begged me not to tell my father. She says he'll go berserk. Apparently he believes that all gays are child molesters as well as AIDS carriers and would be dreadfully upset if he knew the truth.' This is a typical letter, and mentions a typically prejudiced dad who still believes the myth of gays as child molesters. In fact there are far, far fewer gays who assault little boys than heterosexual men who assault little girls.

I get an awful lot of letters from transvestites, too. So many, in fact, that I can hardly go down the street without checking any middle-aged made-up woman twice for stubble under the foundation. Few men seem to know how common transvestism is, nor do they realize that 99 per cent of transvestites are heterosexual, most married with children.

I've always found transvestites interesting since so many write in, and I interviewed one once for a magazine. The circumstances, as so often happens, were much more revealing than the interview itself and summed up how desperately complicated the matter is, not only for transvestites but for those whose lives are involved with them. First of all I approached a transvestites' self-help group and arranged to meet one. A male voice on the end of the phone made an appointment at a hotel and said his name, for the purposes of the interview, would be Gloria Hartwell (or some such name). He said I would recognize him by the fact that he would be wearing a brooch 'fashioned' he said 'like a sea-horse'. A sea-horse is like a masonic handshake in the world of transvestites. They speak silently to each other, sea-horse to sea-horse.

I arrived dreadfully late at the hotel wearing, of all things, trousers. Unable to see anyone remotely like a transvestite in the lobby where I was supposed to meet Gloria, I asked for her at reception. Gloria Hartwell was duly paged and suddenly there appeared before me a lovely young girl with blonde hair and a good figure and bright smile who put out her small, slim hand to me and shook it saying, in a decidedly female voice, 'Gloria Hartwell. What can I do for you?' My suspicions were aroused further by one glaring omission. No brooch fashioned in the shape of a sea-horse.

'I don't think,' I said, staring (I am sure creepily) at her breasts through her blouse and wondering if they were real, 'that you are the person I have come to meet.'

'Well, I haven't got an appointment to meet you,' said Gloria. 'I work here, actually.' I breathed a sigh of relief, thanking my lucky stars I hadn't led her away for a drink and started asking her when she had started to enjoy dressing in women's clothes. 'Who was this lady you wanted to see?'

'We ... ell,' I said, not quite knowing what to say. Luckily the day was saved by an enormous character in a hairy tweed skirt, a purple hat, a brown wig, lyle stockings, clutching a handbag and looking every bit like Charlie's aunt lumbering over to see me.

'Gloria' was a perfect – well, that was the problem – gentleman? As an older woman, should she be allowed to go first through the doors to the bar? Or as a man should he hold the door open for me? Should I allow her to buy me a drink? The fact that I was in trousers seemed to add to the complications.

When we finally sat down and I stammered out my apologies for being late, saying it had been 'one of those days', Gloria gave me a pat on the knee (again, what was I to make of that? Push him away? Or was it just an auntly pat?) and said, in a deep voice: 'One of those days. Don't speak to me about one of those days. You'll never guess what happened to me on the train coming up. I mislaid my vanity bag!'

As one who barely knows what a vanity bag is, let alone owned one, I could only simper in sympathetic but totally hypocritical agreement. Because a vanity bag (presumably a make-up bag) is obviously an essential piece of equipment for the transvestite, while I often go around without wearing make-up at all. The female that 'Gloria' had become was unlike any female I had ever known. And it seems odd that all the transvestites I've ever come across delight in old-fashioned names like Gloria, Gladys, Dolores, Sandra ... names, actually, of their mother's generation. And their clothes are rarely the clothes of today. A great preponderance of transvestites are engineers or army people, people who have to keep up exceptionally male roles in daily life. And there is, interestingly, very little that can be done about the condition. It is a compulsion that hardly any transvestite wants to give up, because it makes them feel so relaxed and secure to feel their feminine side coming out. I rather admired Gloria, for all the Adam's apple and the stubble sticking through the powder and the slightly wonky wig. He had a girlfriend and a job as a plumber and he was very polite and nice, and just as baffled about his condition as I was.

I get letters, too, from men who were sexually abused as children, men who find their daughters attractive and feel dreadfully worried and guilty (even though they've never done anything about it) and letters from men whose girlfriends have been assaulted and who feel consumed with guilt that they didn't protect her, combined with disgust at the fact she's now been tainted, which is followed by disgust with themselves for feeling such disgust.

There is endless variation, it seems, to men's sexual problems. And endless variation to women's too – but they are different problems.

When I was at *Woman*, the letter-answerers would come

in in the morning, take off their coats and make a cup of coffee and sit down to inspect the mail. Then the usual groan would invariably go up. 'Not *another* orgasm letter!' I got so fed up with orgasm letters at *Woman* that eventually I published a letter from a woman which ran along the lines of: 'I have a wonderful sex-life with my husband. I love sex and I look forward to it. But I have never had an orgasm. I feel such a failure. What is the matter with me?'

Impatient with such letters, I wrote what I thought was the last word on the subject. 'If you have a lovely sex-life why complain? Loads of women love sex without orgasm. They love the wonderful feeling of closeness and relaxation, of tenderness and intimacy that comes with love-making. Please don't worry.'

The next post brought a frantic letter. 'Dear Virginia, I have two orgasms every time my husband and I make love, which is every night. But I have never experienced these lovely feelings you talk of like tenderness, intimacy, etc. What is wrong with me?' Rather snappily I wrote back to her saying nothing was wrong with her, that loads of women don't have these feelings, and she should be happy with the orgasms for chrissake.

Orgasms have become dreadful kinds of mountains for women to climb. They talk of 'achieving' them, like promotion. More recently I get letters from women who have a great time in bed but whose partners get angry because they seem to be unable to 'give' them an orgasm. The woman may protest away that she loves sex but the man refuses to believe her. Some men have even given up sex with their girlfriends, much to their unhappiness, because they feel so humiliated at not being able to 'satisfy' their woman. No wonder so many women fake orgasm, just to keep everyone happy. (Faking it is also not thought to be as awful as it used to be. Recently Angela Willans of *Woman's Own* said there was nothing wrong with the occasional 'kindly white lie', which of course it often is.) The trouble is that so many men see sex completely in their own terms and just can't imagine it being any fun to have sex without an orgasm.

Another problem women write in to me about is vaginismus – a tensing of the vaginal muscles, which usually means that penetration is either impossible or extremely painful. I've had women writing in to me who've been married for years without ever having full intercourse and then suddenly want to have a baby. What can they do? Vaginismus is, luckily, one of the sex problems that is easiest to cure, usually with help, and it's nice to be able to point readers in the right direction.

Women write to me worried about their breasts ('like bee-stings' is the common complaint) and vaginal dryness after the menopause, something the doctor never seems to bring up and they're far too embarrassed to broach. They write about funny noises in their vaginas when making love (very common, very embarrassing) and anxieties that their vaginas might be too small for sex, forgetting that since a vagina can expand to let a baby pass through it, it's unlikely to be too small for a penis.

I get very sad letters from women who have suffered sexual abuse – some already middle-aged – some, in writing to me, telling me of the abuse for the first time. I even had a letter from a woman who'd been sexually abused by her father and felt terrible because she *didn't* feel terrible about it. She had quite enjoyed sex with her father, had got married and had a very happy sex-life and was mother to two boys, so what was wrong with her that she didn't feel dirty and guilty? It's difficult to advise someone like this without sounding like one who condones child sexual abuse. My own feeling was not to rock the boat and reassure her that there was nothing odd about her. Everyone deals with these things in different ways. She had obviously dealt with it in a way that worked perfectly well for her. Don't worry.

I even had a letter from a girl who was obsessed with anxiety because she used to play doctors and nurses with her sister. 'I feel so guilty and ashamed. I feel I've done some deep psychological damage and have ruined her life before it's begun. In black moments I contemplate suicide I feel so disgusted with myself.' I tried to reassure her that everyone's played doctors and nurses and she wouldn't have done anyone any harm at all.

And then there are girls who have been raped, also heart-breaking since frequently they have never been for help and have kept the feelings bottled up inside themselves, hoping they'll just go away.

The general sexual worries shared by men and women range far and wide. They are equally susceptible to old wives' tales. They may believe that masturbation makes them blind, that they can't get pregnant standing up, that catching mumps causes infertility, that if they have herpes they'll never be able to have children, that they can't get pregnant while they're having a period, that circumcision will make them last longer, that they'll never get pregnant because when they make love the semen 'all runs out'. (In case any of the above worries anyone, can I repeat that all these assumptions are complete nonsense. They are myths.)

They also share anxieties about AIDS – but I usually get the phobic and obsessional end of the anxieties rather than letters from people who actually have contracted the HIV virus. Someone, for instance, wrote in saying she'd been eating in a restaurant and been offered some olives with specks of red on them. She'd eaten two. Later that night she'd wondered if the specks of red hadn't been blood and whether the chef hadn't got AIDS and cut his finger. Did she now have AIDS?

Another woman wrote saying that the homosexual in their office always made the coffee and used a different cup each time. He often had sores in his mouth (how she knew I don't know). How could she ask him to use his own special cup in future?

Another wrote saying that in the sixties she remembered holding hands with someone who had a cut on his hand covered by a plaster. Now she looked back, it could have slipped. Did she now have AIDS? Since this had occurred to her she had refused sex with her husband and wouldn't touch her children. She could no longer bathe them, or even give them a cuddle or kiss them goodnight. She thought she was going mad.

Another man wrote saying that ten years ago he'd once had sex with a prefect at his boarding school. Did he have AIDS? 'I've always worn a condom since, but now my wife wants children. What shall I do?'

A woman recently wrote saying her husband had bought a second-hand pair of trousers from an Oxfam shop. There were stains around the crotch. He'd worn them once before having them cleaned. Now she was so certain he had AIDS she refused to sleep with him.

And the saddest of all came from a wife who was convinced her husband had AIDS because he seemed tired all the time, he had a sore throat that just wouldn't go away and his hair was thinning on top. She remembered him telling her in the past that he had once been offered a joint at a party and had taken one puff but hated it. I got the sore throat and the tired bit; I even got the bit about the joint (though she'd confused drug-users with intravenous drug-users) but I couldn't understand why the fact her husband was starting to go bald worried her so much. Then I realized she was connecting a symptom of AIDS with a symptom of one of the drugs used to treat the cancer that often results.

Luckily the marvellous AIDS helpline (0800 567123 – it's so good I must put the number in!) copes with all these problems fantastically well.

A common sexual problem is that one or other of the partners wants more sex than the other. The scenario is that she dreads going to bed each night because he'll be pestering her and she doesn't like saying no but really doesn't feel like it. About once a week she gives in. He, on the other hand, is desperately frustrated and feels extremely rejected. One of the solutions to this has been worked out on the lines of new sexual thinking. The couple makes a plan that they will make love on two nights a week, Tuesday and Saturday, say. He promises that he won't pester her on the other days and she promises that they'll make love on those two days. It's an extremely good system which often works very well. He finds twice a week is pretty much enough, and anyway since he knows he's having sex on those two days he feels less stressed generally. She knows she won't be pestered every night so can feel a lot easier. Often couples eventually come to relax the rules and fall into their own satisfactory pattern.

Communication in bed can be a big problem, too. Women tend to imagine their partners are mind-readers and know exactly what they want without saying anything. This is a typical letter I got at *Woman* from a woman with a communication problem.

I'm thirty-six, with a loving husband and a lovely baby boy but after only three years of marriage I'm bored with our love-making. I just can't tell my husband this as I feel I'll hurt him deeply. We don't pet any more before making love so I don't feel satisfied. I spend a lot of the time feeling like crying because of this. We make love a lot – it's just that without some kind of build-up I feel frustrated. I love him so much but I can't go on like this and I'm thinking of leaving.

I replied:

Is it really such a terrible thing to have to mention to him? What would happen if he always forgot to lock the front door when he went out? Would you say you couldn't bear to mention it in case he got hurt? No, you'd tell him that he'd got to remember in future or the house might be burgled. And yet, when your husband is actually forgetting a part of love-making which is very important to you, you don't tell him – even though it seems to be actually putting your whole marriage at risk! And if you can't tell your husband about this, who can you tell? You don't have to be angry and brutal about it. Just say: 'Oh, I did enjoy it the way we used to do it when we petted before we made love – I wish we could do it again sometimes.' Or why not simply make the first move and start petting him?

Then there are the sexual blackmail letters. He wants to try a foursome and says to the wife that if she loved him she'd do it for him. I'm always amazed that wives fall for this illogical argument. They obviously spend nights tossing and turning, convinced that they're bad wives. It never seems to occur to them to reply, using the same logic as their partners: 'If you loved me you wouldn't want me to do something I didn't want to do.'

People often write in with fantasies. My favourite was from a man.

I am writing to you in the hope that you might be able to give me some good advice regarding sexual fantasies. I understand that many people use fantasies but I sometimes feel guilty about my particular fantasy and I am sure it would disgust some people. This fantasy is based around my being a captured spy who is the only person with the answers to some questions, and I use this to justify what my fantasy captors do to me. Because I refuse to answer the questions, my captors 'interrogate' me using ALL the methods of the Gestapo and the current-day South American countries. There is no need for further detail; suffice it to say that in my fantasy my captors, having made me suffer horrendously at their hands, invariably make me talk. Despite the fact that torture is clearly an evil solution, in my fantasy I am on the 'bad' side and my captors are the 'good' people. As a stimulant I use real and fictional accounts of these acts being carried out. However, it seems somehow wrong that these people, some of whom have given their lives to make the world a better and safer place to live in, should provide me with gratification in this manner. This seems particularly wrong in view of the fact that I am only thirty-two and have a heart condition which would almost certainly kill me if I were to be actually tortured in this way. I am not sure whether I have explained myself clearly, but I hope that you can understand my problem.

Women have fantasies, too. Many have fantasies of being raped, though they'd rather die than anyone unwelcome so much as make a pass at them. Some just have the normal fantasies of everyday life – and feel so guilty they almost want to kill themselves. 'My marriage is very good – in fact so good that I sometimes wonder if something won't come along to spoil it,' a reader wrote to me at *Woman* ...

> But I'm desperate for reassurance that I'm not perverted. It's just that I have worrying thoughts about other men. Or rather, one man in particular. It started when I accidentally touched his hand. Then he came to stay the night in the spare room and when I changed the sheets the next day I caught myself thinking: what if he were here now and I jumped on him and we made love? I just can't see myself ever doing that, so why think it? And I had my fringe cut the other day and when I got out of the hairdresser's I thought: what if he saw me now? I feel so dreadfully guilty. I feel I ought to leave my husband and that I'm a worthless person. Most of the time my thoughts are perfectly normal.

I replied that in fact *all* of the time her thoughts were perfectly normal and the only thing not normal about her was the fact that she felt guilty about them. 'If we could all read each other's thoughts, none of us would be speaking to each other, you know!' I wrote. 'And if you're worried about *your* thoughts, I hope you never find out some of the weird things I think about!'

Then there was the letter from the prostitute who gave it all up for a steady man. 'The problem is I've lost all sexual feeling. I feel terribly self-conscious which seems ridiculous considering my past. Could it be that I've given up working – after all, it seems pointless when in the past I could earn in a couple of hours what would take me a week now.'

I suggested that her problem was simply a case of change. 'Imagine a faithful housewife suddenly being flung into a life of prostitution; don't you think she'd find herself completely confused by what she was doing? Isn't it rather the same with you? You've never experienced permanence and you're having to learn an awful lot in a very short space of time. You don't slip into enjoying fidelity and exclusive relationships naturally – it's all a matter of learning as you go along. Indeed you may never learn, but I think you will slowly.' This girl, who'd written anonymously, wrote to me after seeing her letter in print saying what a difference my advice had made.

I get letters from couples wondering about the legality of taking nude photographs. There's nothing wrong with it, but the best thing is to take them on Polaroid cameras. If the pictures aren't absolutely straightforward, there's always the risk that you may run into problems because the Post Office Act makes it an offence to send indecent material through the post, meaning the print might not be returned to you because the developer could be charged. Most developers wouldn't take the risk and would ask you to collect them personally – or they'd conveniently 'lose' them in processing.

I get letters about sex from people everywhere, and all ages, too. One of the most delightful was from an elderly lady:

> I'm eighty and my husband is eighty-four. I've always been interested to know why some people make lots of noise when they make love. Is it a class thing? Is it done only in the slums by rough people but not by the gentry or nobility? Or is it a matter of emotional temperament and done by people at all levels of society? I heard a radio play recently and there was a Spanish couple making love and he was roaring and she was screaming! Surely noisy sex must cause embarrassment to other people? What happens in hotels? Don't children hear? I'm not in the least a prude but it seems to me a bit vulgar to let one's love-making be heard!

I replied:

> Lots of people are noisy when making love and lots aren't. It's

dependent on what sort of people they are, not what class they are. It can be annoying for neighbours and embarrassing in hotels, which is why noisy lovers don't particularly enjoy staying in them because they feel they have to keep things down a bit. As far as the radio play goes, do remember that the radio depends on sound. It'd be rather difficult to convey a sex scene with a couple of completely silent partners, wouldn't it? After all, the sound of bed-springs twanging wouldn't quite give the listeners the impression of steaming sex, would it?

Certainly agony aunts are often surprised by some of the letters they get on the subject of sex. But sometimes readers have been surprised at the response they've got from agony aunts. When Deidre Sanders mentioned on the page that a woman had experienced orgasm for the first time in her life after having read her leaflet *Women and Orgasm*, literally thousands of *Sun* readers wrote in asking for a copy of the leaflet. For some reason Deidre's address had been missed on that particular column so the readers thumbed through the paper to find an address, which happened to be the office, just down the road from the main editorial office, which despatched the *Sun*'s bingo cards. Deidre was soon flooded with letters from readers complaining: 'I sent for your leaflet on orgasm and you sent me a bingo card. What on earth am I supposed to do with that?'

Agony columns get so many problems about sex because there really is nowhere else that most people feel able to turn. That's why I think our responsibility is so particularly important. It's specially important not to get sex out of proportion, not to make anyone feel guilty about not having enough sex or envious that their sex life isn't good enough. People are extremely vulnerable in this area and the more reassurance they can get, the better. A reply telling them how to have an orgasm isn't nearly as reassuring as a reply which says they're absolutely normal not to have an orgasm – plus a leaflet that explains how to have one if they want, of course.

My own feeling is that if you tell someone that sex once a fortnight lasting two minutes is a lot more sex than some men are capable of (plus a leaflet on sex therapy if they want it) it is more likely to make them feel more manly and sexy than saying: 'Cripes, only two minutes only once a fortnight, boy have you got problems!'

And anyway, why worry quite so much about sex? Sex isn't the most important thing in the world. Reading sex books you often get the impression that sex is on everyone's mind all the time, day and night. On the bus, in the tube, they may be pretending to read their evening papers, but really they're just imagining sex, sex and more sex! This may be true of lusty teenagers but hardly true of the rest of us.

Books often recommend going off with your partner for a sexy weekend to revive flagging desire. In the early days of a relationship, fine. But the old man you've spent the last fifteen years of your life with? Could you really spend forty-eight hours in bed together? Maybe you could spend an hour in bed, but what about the next forty-seven? Sex can't change your life. It can't give you intimacy or love in a loveless relationship. It's a bonus, icing on the cake, not a be-all and end-all. It's worth getting sex into proper perspective and remembering that if we make love for, say, five minutes twice a week, then in a year we'll have spent less than nine hours a year actually having sex. Okay, okay, that's not fair, is it? There's the build-up and the cosy cuddle afterwards and so on. All right. Make it half an hour. Four hours a month. Or, if you like, even eight hours. Whatever, compared to the time you spend together chatting, rubbing along, watching telly, giggling, planning and so on, it's not an awfully long time. And although it's important, it really should be put into its proper perspective.

* * * *

'Lucky,' says the Blazer, 'that I have no problems in that

department. What was it that Claire Rayner called it? Trigger trouble?

The Computer Programmer is going redder and redder and groping, for some reason, for his wallet. I notice he has taken a card from it, which he holds half-hidden in his hand.

'The baby,' I say, starting to rise. 'If I stay jabbering on any longer, that baby will be a teenager by the time I get to give him his teddy.'

'He's been put down,' says the Motherly Woman, who is passing by with a heap of sandwiches she has rustled up off her own bat.

The Computer Programmer jumps. 'Put down?' he says, looking aghast. 'Oh, you mean …'

'Put to bed. He's tired with all these people and all this racket,' says the Motherly Woman. 'Why she wanted to have a party when she's ever so tired and needs her sleep, I just don't know.'

'Oh, any excuse,' says the Blazer. 'Anyway, we've been hearing all about the problem page. And all about trigger trouble.'

'Trigger trouble?' says the Motherly Woman. 'Surely you don't get letters about guns, dear?' Then she catches on and looks horrified. She retrieves herself by saying, 'What worries me is all those people who write in and you don't put them on the page. What happens to them'

'I answer them,' I say, holding out my paper cup for a top-up from the Blazer.

'But surely,' says the Motherly Woman, relieved of her sandwich plate by the Neighbour's Partner who makes a face at it, 'surely you don't reply to all of them?'

'You Surely Don't Reply to All of Them?'

Every letter that comes in to the problem page gets a personal reply. Those that get answered on the page get a personal reply. Those that don't come with stamped addressed envelopes get personal replies. Even those that are virtually unreadable get personal replies. I feel it's only right that for the problems and dilemmas that make up the page, a paper or magazine should repay its debt by giving something back to those people who write in.

Before I arrived at *Woman* I never realized what an amazing service problem pages offer. I never realized either, come to that, what an awful lot of work there was to do, and that about ninety per cent of an agony aunt's job is behind the scenes. And what a huge responsibility it is.

The sheer dreary labour is enough to start with. Daily, the post has to be opened, stamped and counted. The letters are read and then sent out to the letter-answerers, who record the replies on tape and return them to my secretary who types them up. Each reply is usually accompanied by one of my hundred or so leaflets, each with loads of addresses and sources of help on it. (These leaflets have to be photocopied, sorted and kept up to date by yearly checking, a mammoth task in itself.) Finally, every envelope has to be stuffed and sent out. If there's been a particularly interesting leaflet featured on the page that week, like a sex leaflet or one on loneliness or depression, there might easily be over two hundred leaflets alone to be dealt with a day. When we offered a collection of 'Words of Wisdom' and 'Words of Comfort', the requests came in in their thousands.

Not every agony aunt works for a publication that can afford the service of answering letters privately. But I find the practice of not replying reprehensible – just a matter of making money and copy out of people's misery without giving anything in return. But write to Deidre Sanders, Marje Proops, Barbara Jackson, Claire Rayner, Gill Cox, Angela Willans, Anne Lovell, Suzie Hayman, and many others, and they will all reply with a personal letter.

Of those agony aunts who don't reply, some don't because their companies can't afford it, some don't because they can't be bothered, and Irma Kurtz doesn't on principle.

'When you make this sort of thing a profession you're in danger,' she says. 'The risk of pity, of getting big on other people's troubles, is great. I don't even like needing other people's troubles financially to pay my way. Which is why I'm glad that agony aunting is only a fraction of my income. The danger is that you come to depend on and need people's troubles and you lose the dream. And the dream is an ideal world full of untroubled people. Depending on other people's troubles might make you think you do have an answer. And the main thing to remember being an agony aunt is that you haven't got an answer. You only have a different viewpoint on the problem.

'So I only reply personally in emergencies – abortion, violence, drugs. I don't like the idea of making a cottage industry of other people's pain.'

My particular 'cottage industry' first involves reading all the letters that have come in and making suitable comments, if necessary, at the top. Many's the letter which I've peppered with red-penned comments like: 'What a creep!' 'I don't believe it!' 'How can she stay with him!' 'What about the son?' 'See a solicitor at once!' 'There but for the grace of

God ...' and so on. (I was happily scrawling such incredulous comments over one until, to my horror, I came to a PS at the end of the letter: 'Please send this letter back to me so I can show it to my husband. Reading it through, I see that it expresses so much better how I feel than I can ever say to him out loud.' The Tipp-Ex had to be used far into the night on that one.)

The letters that I answer entirely myself are the ones that refer to my answers on the page, ones that strike a particular chord or which are particularly urgent – involving, say, child-cruelty, suicide threats or abortion. I also answer as many as possible with the aid of a leaflet and a yellow slip on which I scrawl, in unreadable writing, notes of sympathy, brief suggestions and perhaps a useful address.

The work just has to be cut down in this way because whenever a publisher is snooping around looking for cuts, his scissors invariably hover over the reader-service department. When I arrived at *Woman* in the seventies, for instance, it boasted a Reader Service Department with twelve full-time letter-answerers for the whole magazine. There was a Head of the Reader Service Department and even one person employed solely as a 'Signer', whose job was to check the letters and sign them all before they went out! Four of these staff spent their time exclusively on the letters to the problem page. When I left I had only one letter-answerer to help me.

When I arrived, my offices were sited well away from this department and the letters were brought round to my office in the morning in a folder by the Chief Problem-Page Letter-Answerer. I was not made particularly welcome in the Reader Service Department at first and the idea of my reading the personal answers that were going out in my name was rather discouraged. All the letters were answered and signed on my behalf by the Chief Letter-Answerer. I was having none of that. I soon insisted that all the answers were shown to me and I wouldn't let any go out until I was satisfied that the answers were correct – at least correct in my eyes (which obviously begs a lot of questions, but still). To make certain, I signed every one, taking full responsibility for each answer that went out and I have continued to do so. Like most other agony aunts, I do this because I feel that if people are writing in to me personally with their problems it is only right and good-mannered to respond personally as well. They are writing to me, and they must hear back from me.

But it's physically impossible for me actually to compose every answer myself, so at the *Sunday Mirror*, after I've sorted through the letters, they're sent off to my three letter-answerers. They're all women with small children and counselling experience, who answer the letters into a tape-recorder. The tapes are then returned to my secretary who types them.

Then it's back to me. I check through them to see that I'm signing letters that I can stand by.

It must be a difficult job answering letters for someone else, and up to a point my letter-answerers all have to be mind-readers. Although I only employ people who are reasonably like-minded, obviously no one can think in quite the same way as another. Also, people do get facts wrong – as I am sure I have done myself – and people do have off-days. We all have personal prejudices and bees in our bonnets. And while many of my bees are shared by others, it's not usual to find people who share whole hives.

My own particular bonnet has the following bees:

- Since there is a difference between right and wrong, I don't hesitate to make it clear now and again. When a panel of agony aunts was asked by a member of an audience at some do or other whether they ever told their readers what they 'should' do, the other two with me piously said that it would be unthinkable to do such a thing. Readers would have to make up their own minds. It wasn't our place to make judgements. Non-directive advice was the only way. I disagreed strongly. I said I thought it was wrong to break the law, to hurt others, to treat children and animals cruelly, to cheat on your loved ones, to bring unwanted children into the world ... and so on. I also think it helps people to use morality as a yardstick for their behaviour. But since I also think it's wrong to hurt people or make them feel small and lowly, there's no way that I would deliver truth unkindly in a letter to anyone or make the person feel worthless and immoral. There are ways and ways of delivering the truth, but if it is the truth and sincerely felt then the hurt the recipient may feel is, I hope, assuaged by the fact that only a good friend would be so honest with them.

- I am perhaps keener than most on women having the freedom to choose abortion – on the grounds that while it may be wrong to abort a foetus (I don't think it is) it is very wrong to bring an unwanted child into the world.

- I'm frightfully po-faced about affairs with married people if they have children.

- I constantly urge, in divorce cases, that unless the child is particularly terrified or miserable about seeing the departed parent, he or she should be encouraged to see him or her as much as possible.

- Children, if there are any, should nearly always take priority. I've got no time for people who think of children as 'little horrors'; no time for parents who have children and then don't consider their feelings as No. 1 on the agenda. They didn't ask to be born, is my view, and you can never teach a child to care and be considerate if you don't behave the same to it yourself.

- If any single person writes asking about AID (Artificial Insemination by Donor) as a means of getting pregnant without a father being around, I always send them the information but with a strong disapproving letter accompanying it – I just don't think it's right to plan to have a baby without a father on the scene at all. To agree with a male friend to have a child and for him to agree to play the role of father even though he doesn't live with you, is one thing; but to go out coldly and just grab any old sperm is surely the ultimate in selfishness. The child loses out on a father, a whole set of grandparents and relations and is only half as lucky as a child with both. No way to start your life, though I know that in some cases it is inevitable later on – in which case, one has to make the best of it, as indeed, I have done myself.

- My views on full-time working mums are frightfully unfashionable, probably because I was the daughter of a wildly successful career woman and brought up a lot of the time by au pairs. It is no fun. Why have children if you only bring them up at weekends?
- A man can't blame a girl for getting pregnant if he hasn't used a condom even if she swears she's on the Pill. A girl can't blame a man for getting her pregnant even if his condom splits. Over the years I have learnt that the only person you can really trust is yourself.
- And finally I attach rather less importance to sex than most people, despite the fact that I get an awful lot of letters on the subject.

As I hear my voice rising to a shrill scream at this moment, and can feel my eyes starting to bulge and the hair waving frantically around as it comes away from the pins at the back, I notice the Blazer shifting from foot to foot. He gestures politely that he is leaving but coming back and I have no doubt he is off to fetch the men in white coats. The Computer Programmer, however, is still stuck with me, so I address the rest of my lecture to him. I have a feeling he wants to catch me alone for a second, but he can wait till I've finished.

As I have bees in my bonnet, so others have bees, naturally, in theirs. And most letter-writers have a few buzzing around, whose right to buzz I have always felt I have had to respect – particularly as angry bees sting. I inherited a letter-writer who was a Catholic, for instance, who refused to write letters recommending anyone had an abortion or get divorced – quite understandable, of course, but you can imagine she wasn't able to answer that number of letters.

I had a temporary letter-writer who felt strongly that she had to answer the letters in a completely personal way. The fact that they were being signed by me seemed to make no difference to her. Her letters would run on the lines of: 'I am so sorry about your fear of flying and that you are so anxious about your proposed holiday to Gibraltar. But if you do manage to overcome it by contacting one of the organizations on my phobia leaflet then do go along to a marvellous bar on the main street (it's left of the church) and introduce yourself to Bob and Greg who run it. They'll tell you about all the sights, they do a wonderful *paella* (that's one of Spain's national dishes and an absolute must!) and their prices are very reasonable.' Those letters had to be re-written, needless to say. Though they have a certain direct charm.

And it's true that because we agony aunts are already a bit more distant physically we can afford to get closer to people emotionally in a letter without the fear of getting too involved. I was touched to read the answer an agony aunt gave in the *East Caribbean Times* to a girl who was terribly depressed and desperate for a job to pay off her debts. She got right down to business after saying how deeply she felt for her plight, and added: 'There's a Kenneth Skinner at Upper Wavel Ave. Black Rock who is looking for someone to live at home to help his wife. He has promised that that person would be treated like any member of the family. Drop him a note and see if his offer is still open.' There is something so utterly frank and friendly about that reply that I almost feel ashamed of myself for not daring to come up with the practical goods more often. What therapist would ever offer such help and advice? They would only lean back in their chairs and ask why the girl was depressed and why she felt she needed a job and so on ... undoubtedly useful in some cases but not all.

The problem with answering letters quite so specifically is

that it can lead to danger. What if Kenneth Skinner turned out to be a rapist, for instance? I managed to snatch back a reply done by another letter-answerer before it went out. She answered a lonely girl in London: 'I suggest you go along to a pub opposite the Brompton Oratory one evening. It's called the Bunch of Grapes and if you hang around there long enough you'll be sure to bump into some nice young man who has a couple of theatre tickets and who will ask you along.' The nightmare scenario for the girl was, of course, that she would be found stabbed and raped in an alleyway. The nightmare scenario for me was that my incriminating letter would be found in her handbag.

Another letter-writer was once married to a bi-sexual which made her, rightly, particularly sensitive to letters about AIDS. She refused, again rightly in her own eyes, to answer letters in the way I wanted at the time (which was to respond to anyone who had had a petting session with a Spaniard with a cut on his hand, or who had had a one-night stand in 1977, in a totally reassuring way). I would insist on writing that there was no chance at all that the person who wrote in circumstances like these could possibly have AIDS. My letter-writer could not bring herself to write anything but 'If you are worried, have an AIDS test'.

One letter-writer developed the habit of ending her letters: 'Be happy, love and cherish yourself, be good to yourself' – phrases I discouraged because I've always felt that that particular piece of advice is one of the most useless and unhelpful. Indeed, when anyone has ever said to me, in parting, 'Goodbye and take care of yourself' (there was a fashion for such a phrase in the seventies), I always felt there was an unspoken coda which ran: 'Because no one else will!'

Bees are easier to deal with than sudden blind-spots. More recently a perfectly sensible letter-answerer suggested withdrawal as a method of contraception, and on another occasion suggested to a reader who wrote about his premature ejaculation that he try making love more than once a night. 'By the third time you may well find your problem has lessened.' My eyes were popping at the idea of this poor guy receiving a letter encouraging him to make love three times in a night! It was interesting that the letter-answerer had never suggested such a method before. And also interesting that the reader was black. I couldn't help wondering if she didn't have some subconscious messages on the 'all black guys are incredibly sexy' lines whizzing around under her radical exterior. I'm sure she would have been horrified if she'd re-read the letter properly.

The other sort of letter that I always retrieve and re-write is the one that makes the reader even more worried than when she wrote. I had one letter from a woman with a cancer phobia. She wrote that she had had yearly smears, regularly checked her breasts, that her family had no history of cancer, that no one in her family smoked or drank, that her doctor had given her a thorough going over and she had had a recent blood test which was clear – but she was still terrified that she had cancer. 'I worry myself sick about it,' she wrote. 'What can you do to help me?'

The letter-writer (who was having an off-day – normally she was marvellous) wrote back: 'I am so sorry to hear of your fear of cancer. I can assure you that if what you tell me is true, that you have had all these tests, that your doctor has reassured you and that there is no history of cancer in your family, there is no way that you have cancer. So please do stop worrying. *Because if there is one sure way to get cancer it is to worry too much*. Doctors are now certain that stress and cancer are inextricably linked ...' and so on.

This same letter-writer liked to spell the word 'affair' 'affaire'. I tried in vain to insist she spelt it the way I preferred but she had a thing about this spelling and in the end I didn't have the heart to persist and just laboriously and privately altered the word in Tipp-Ex when I couldn't stand it. I always imagine 'affaires' to be rather grand and glamorous things and certainly many of the grubby capers my readers got up to could hardly be termed 'affaires'. Indeed, many hardly merited the word 'affair'. ('Wham bam thank-you mam' could also contravene the Trades Descriptions Act since many of the incidents were little more than a 'bam' with no such foreplay as 'wham', let alone any after-sex courtesies.)

But these are the daily niggles of letter-answering that can usually be easily dealt with by PSs or correction fluid; I quote them only to show what a very different art letter-writing is from replying to someone face-to-face. Anything you write is there, on paper. It can't be taken back. The desperately unhappy woman who'd been married thirty years to a man who'd had a mild flirtation with his secretary, though he had never slept with her, and had begged his wife's forgiveness, would not have been happy with the reply she might have got if I hadn't tinkered with the letter first: 'Please put this aside. Many men in mid-life want to feel they are still attractive and the reason he had this flirtation is probably due to a rather pathetic insecurity prompted by his age. It was nothing. And I'm sure he didn't sleep with her. Though that doesn't mean to say that he wouldn't have wanted to had the relationship continued.' No prize for guessing which sentence would leap out at that poor woman from the page, haunt her and eat away at her heart. *'Though that doesn't mean to say he wouldn't have wanted to....'* In the middle of the night she would wake up, heart pounding, and scan the letter to make sure I really had written it. Yes I had. It was true.

You can't retract what you've written, you can't even claim never to have said it. It's down there in writing and you have to be very careful that what you say is what you mean and that what you say is true and that what you say isn't going to make the reader worry more.

It's important, therefore, never to say anything that criticizes past actions on the lines of: 'It's a pity you spoke so hastily to your mother-in-law. If only you'd kept your trap shut! No wonder she refuses you speak to you! You say you want to make it up, but you should have thought of this before you opened your big mouth!' Much better to write: 'Most people with difficult mothers-in-law can well sympathize with how you felt and what you said. You would have to have had the patience of Job not to have responded as you did. However, I can understand how hurt she was and obviously you're wondering now how can you repair the damage.' And so on.

The reply to a man who left his wife in a fit of temper and now can't be reconciled, should not be: 'Although I think you're right and perhaps you shouldn't have left your wife, now you must look to the future.' There is absolutely no reason to write that first phrase down. If he shouldn't have left his wife then don't mention it. Get on to the future straight away. It's often helpful to suggest that people look at these incidents as firmly set in the past where they belong. Rather than mull over some past disastrous incident along with the reader, compare what happened to a sight passed long ago in a speeding car. The future is what to concentrate on now, not the past.

Similarly, if someone is writing saying they got drunk in the early months of pregnancy there's no point in saying, 'Many women who drink heavily in pregnancy risk their babies suffering from foetal alcohol syndrome. But as this was a one-off so you probably have no cause to be worried.' Foetal alcohol syndrome? Worse, that word 'probably'? It's enough to make anyone rush to the bottle. (By the way, just in case anyone's reading this who's pregnant, and got totally pissed last night, the latest research shows that there is only real cause to worry about drinking in pregnancy if you are an extremely heavy, *regular* drinker.)

There is a variety of rules that apply when answering problem letters. Foremost of these comes speed. It really is important to write back as soon as you can. Speed is more important than anything – content, spelling, whatever. When people are low, they wait for the postman from the moment they put their letter in the box.

Having got down to answering the letter promptly, the next step is to read the letter thoroughly, including the address. Many is the letter I've spent quite a time replying to, and it's only when writing the envelope that I've realized that the person has written from a secure ward at Rampton, for instance. The entire letter has to be re-written. If the person is writing from a hostel, a prison, a hospital bed – it all makes a difference to how one might reply.

Then, it's worth taking in the handwriting and vocabulary and trying to get a feeling of the person who's written the letter, something that most people do instinctively. Are they elderly? Are they educated? Letter-writers try, up to a point, to tailor their replies to the sort of person who's written in, bearing in mind that older people sometimes have different views and values from younger people. For instance, if a woman of sixty-eight writes in having had a drunken one-night stand with a seventy-year-old (such things do happen) it would probably not be appropriate to suggest that in future she always insists her partners take precautions because of the risk of AIDS.

How readers sign themselves is quite revealing, too. Although most people address me as 'Dear Virginia' (though some are more formal with 'Dear Miss Ironside') it's more interesting to see whether they sign themselves 'Bob' or 'Mr B. Barker'. You don't want to reply to a 'Bob' as 'Mr Barker' or vice-versa.

I always go through letters with a highlighter pen to make sure I don't miss anything out. Sometimes I'll look at letter-writers' replies and find that they've missed one question; quite often it's the stupidest but also the most crucial, like the girl who wrote as a PS to her letter: 'I also wondered if sex could have been painful because I'm very short and my boyfriend was very tall.' These sorts of questions may seem slightly dotty but actually this one was probably a persistent niggle and something that she dared not ask anyone else about. I'm sure we all have funny little questions like that which wander about in our heads; and when readers ask us, it's always important to reply to them, however loopy they seem. And if people write in with questions I don't know the answer to, it's better, rather than to ignore them, to admit one hasn't a clue and suggest further sources of help.

If someone ends their letter with the words: 'I feel such a stupid, small-minded, rotten person for saying all this but it's made me feel better for writing it down,' she doesn't want to get back a letter that starts: 'Thank you for your letter. I don't think you're a stupid, small-minded, rotten person.' That sort of talk is for conversation, and not stuff for the typewriter. She shouldn't be reminded of these feelings of loathing. The words 'small-minded, rotten and stupid' shouldn't even *appear* in the letter back. At least not in relation to the person who's writing – her enemies, perhaps!

I often find it's useful to look at the writer's problem and précis it for him or her, giving short summaries of what the options are. For instance: 'You seem to be married to a very difficult man and are in a dilemma about what to do. What are the options? You could leave him, stay with him, live with him but have separate lives, go for counselling and help first before deciding to leave him if you still feel like it – or you could always continue as you are.' It's often worth putting this last in as an option because people forget that doing nothing is sometimes the best way of dealing with a situation and if you list it as a course of action, it makes doing nothing seem a positive choice rather than a passive state of affairs.

You can see from this that the letters that go out to people personally are very different to the answers on the page. They're much longer, for a start, usually about a page long, and this way I'm able to give a much more comprehensive answer, usually full of 'on the one hand and on the other hand' sort of things that would become boring if repeated too often in the paper.

It may sound Pollyanna-ish, but I always like to end letters on a kind note like 'I am thinking of you' or 'You are in my thoughts and I look forward to hearing how you are getting on. Please keep in touch.'

Finally I always find it's best, if possible, to look through the letter after I've written it. How does it sound now? Have I answered all the points? Does the letter have a strong spine to it, is it like a rock for someone to cling to or is it a bit wet and over-sympathetic? And have I been truthful, positive and sensitive throughout? While it's right to be extremely sympathetic and never demean anyone's misery, it's worth avoiding phrases like 'I don't think you'll be unhappy for the rest of your life'. (This is usually in answer to someone who's written: 'I think I'll be unhappy for the rest of my life' and who has probably forgotten he's written that precise phrase when he gets the reply.) The weakness of this reply lies in the words 'I don't think' which imply 'you might' and only add fuel to the recipient's depression. It's much better to write, instead: 'You sound such a strong and warm person, I know that you will get through this dreadful patch,' or something on those lines (as long, of course, as it seems true).

When new technology arrived on the scene, inevitably the thought crossed my mind of answering letters in pre-written blocks. It was a great idea – you'd press Paste 1, and, presto, a whole paragraph about Relate would appear. Paste 2 would produce a description of phobias and Paste 3 would deal with jealousy. Of course, although a riveting parlour game, it never got to the stage of even being tried out. It was obvious it wouldn't work: the letters are from people, and you can't answer people with ready-made paragraphs.

The idea is still an entertaining one, however. Pamela Branch wrote a hilarious description of how it could be done in her thriller, *Murder's Little Sister* (Robert Hale, 1958). An agony aunt has jumped out of a window, leaving her colleagues to sort out the complicated procedure she had worked out for answering the problem letters. This procedure involves numerous large charts and two lengths of string. The charts cover an enormous variety of premises, characteristics, complications and answers; one end of each string is placed on a chart relevant to the problem in question, and where the strings cross the answer would, in theory, reveal itself.

On testing her system, one of her colleagues came up with the following:

'I am a refugee, travelling on a Turkish laissez-passez, I went through a form of marriage in 1942 with a passing soldier. He went off at once. I have not seen him since. Anyway, he was a Mormon and only had a Mexican divorce from his first wife. I got an affidavit from a man in Tiflis and have since married him. He is a Muslim and very cruel to me. He has five wives all living in the same house. My first husband's divorced wife has now married my present husband. Are our children any relation?'

We see how this breaks down when the answer comes out: ' "If you will send me a stamped addressed envelope I will reply privately." '

It's a pity the system would never work in real life. As it is, some letters need even more special handling than others. Obviously we get our fair share of cranks writing in, usually in red or green ink. Sometimes people are mentally ill. It's very distressing to get an extremely concerned and anxious letter from someone who is convinced, say, that their television is bugged by Martians or that messages are coming through the radiators or that their neighbours are listening in to everything they say through the walls. It's no use telling them they are suffering from a mental illness or that it's all in their minds. The best thing is to recommend they visit their doctor urgently, saying their problem is very common and that doctors have special ways of dealing with television sets, radiators or neighbours like theirs. This is not, of course, strictly true, but my feeling is that it's vital to get them to their doctors come what may because it may well be that with the help of drugs they can be made a great deal happier and often get back to normal, the voices and messages silenced.

Both Claire Rayner and Deidre Sanders put exceptionally troubled letters into a special file and follow them up. (After interviewing Claire and Deidre for this book, I now do the same.) They will write, after three weeks or so, saying: 'You don't have to reply if you don't want to but I just wondered how you were.'

'It makes a big difference,' says Claire. 'Very often things have been resolved; but very often things are the same but they feel better for getting a letter.'

Now and again she gets involved financially. 'Oh yes, one woman wrote, very upset that she couldn't afford a headstone for one of her children who had died. I talked to my features editor and between us all we sent her the money for the stone and she since has had a normal healthy child and we remain in touch. I also chuck the odd fiver into a letter now and again, but then you do, don't you? I shouldn't do it but sometimes I can't bear it.'

What we don't often get is a chance to read other agony aunts' personal replies. One way or another, though, I've read a few, most of which sound perfectly good. But once a reader wrote to me, extremely upset to have received a reply from the agony aunt on another paper. She had written to this particular agony aunt saying she had been married for two years to a man ten years older than herself. For the last year he had spent his free time sitting in front of the telly, eating; he complained that she let the house go, though she cleaned her house thoroughly twice a week. Her husband made most of the mess. She was a big girl, but her husband had always said he would hate it if she were slim; her problem was his lack of attention. Although he said he loved her constantly, he never helped with the housework; if they made love in the early evening he insisted that the telly stayed on throughout so he didn't miss the beginning of *Crossroads*.

The only time she felt she loved him was when she imagined him dead.

She sent me a copy of the letter she got back from the agony aunt (whom I won't name). It said, in part:

> Your husband has the burden and worry of working to keep you and your home and making sure all the bills are paid and that the household is running smoothly. This, in itself, is enough for a man to do ... You cannot expect a man to know how to cook, iron or clean a house ... it is your responsibility to see that the home is kept in pristine condition ... why not be a little more house-proud? All men are untidy (unless they are prissy) ... You say you are fourteen stones. Why not get back that sylph-like figure which I am sure you used to have? Most men do not like overweight women and I wonder if that is why he is not so keen on taking you out any more. It is something which you can do something about with a little discipline and always be well dressed and well made-up even if you are only going to lounge at home. It creates a right impression ... Your parents adore him and think he is getting a rough deal from you. Do you think they could be right? ... I have a feeling that if you could get your priorities right, your marriage has a lot going for it. Please try because the woman is always the homemaker — whatever the women's libbers think or say.

And so on. This was in 1985. For me it breaks every rule in the book. It's a letter that would make the person who wrote in feel small and lowly and ever so much worse than before. She is blamed for everything. No wonder the poor woman wrote to me for a second opinion!

Having said all this, however, I don't want it to sound as if letter-writers are dreadful people who are always making mistakes. Generally the standard of the letter-writers I've had is incredibly high; I'm often really proud to sign my name to their offerings. Many is the time I think how lucky I am to have such good ones and marvel at some twist or perception that's appeared in the answer that I'd never have thought of myself. (Many's the time I've nicked some particularly pithy insight of theirs and used it in an answer on the page.) And I can't help feeling proud that two of my letter-answerers have gone on to become agony aunts themselves – Anne Lovell for *Bella* and Maroushka Monro for *Just Seventeen*.

Difficult as it may seem to answer letters on behalf of someone else, there's one thing that makes it easier. The letters themselves. These often seem to dictate their own replies and nine times out of ten the answer – to anyone with common sense, a kind heart and a bit of wisdom – is so obvious that you could get people of all different ages, races, religions and nationalities answering a particular letter and I've no doubt their answers would be much of a muchness. And if you take on staff who are reasonably like-minded and sympathetic, your chances of getting a reply you'll go along with are even higher.

The *Sunday Times Magazine* did a fascinating experiment a few years ago. They composed a problem letter supposedly from a woman who was unhappily married to a hospital consultant and had fallen in love with one her husband's medical students. This affair was trundling along when the medical student gave her an ultimatum – either leave her husband and live with him or he'd take a job abroad and never see her again. The problem was that although he liked one of the children who was fourteen, he wasn't too keen on the other, younger boy, who was partially deaf. What should she do?

They sent this letter to agony aunts around the world to see what their differing replies would be. America, Sweden, South Africa, Japan, Italy and France all advised, in one way or another, that she should leave with her lover. Australia, Eire and the UK, after outlining the alternatives, said she had to make up her own mind and be more her own woman. But none said she should stay. It certainly makes one realize that however much one may pride oneself on one's own good and sensible advice, caring advice from almost any source is probably much of a muchness.

*   *   *   *

The Computer Programmer is clearly in distress. Something is on his mind and has been for a while. I take pity on him.

'Your card?' I say, *extracting the now rather damp and squishy rectangle that he has been toying with all through my last monologue.*

'Well, must move these sandwiches around,' says the Motherly Woman, *looking round for her plate.* 'Now where are they?'

She bustles off in search of them while I put the Computer Programmer out of his misery.

'Would you like me to send you one of my leaflets?' I say. 'Just for a laugh?'

The relief that courses through the Computer Progammer is tangible.

'Only if you have the time,' he says. 'I mean ...'

'I'll send you Loneliness, Depression, Phobias and ...' *unkind pause ...* 'Men's Sex Problems and Sex Therapy.'

'Just for a laugh,' he says.

'Of course,' I say. 'Just so you can have a good old giggle, eh?'

'Thank you,' he says. *He pauses. He picks at a crisp. Someone the other side of the room is saying goodbye to the Neighbour but the party is still going strong. Ashtrays are overflowing; now someone has closed the garden doors and drawn the curtains. The Motherly Woman is starting to collect glasses but the Neighbour is coming out of the kitchen with two new bottles of wine.*

'How much good do you think you do?' *asks the Computer Programmer, earnestly.* 'I mean, what use, if you'll forgive me, is just a letter?'

'What Use Is Just a Letter?'

When writing in to the problem page, much of the help people get is from themselves. The actual act of writing their problem down is enormously useful. Writing helps concentrate the mind; trying to convey it on paper forces the writer to clarify the problem. What exactly is it that they are worried about? The whole problem has to be defined.

There is therapy, too, in getting everything off your chest. And it could be, too, that, the letter has a symbolic role: write your problems on a piece of paper, stick them in an envelope and post them off, and they are now separate from you, chucked away into a void. I don't think this is entirely true, but at least writing the problem down separates it from the rest of you. Instead of being a worried person, you are a person with a worry.

So just writing the problem down makes lots of people feel better automatically. Many is the letter I've had that has ended with the words: 'Well, thanks for just being there, anyway. I feel so much better for writing it down.' And often readers say, interestingly: 'Now I look back on my letter I think I know what your answer is going to be.' Sometimes they look back on their letter and ask for me to return it to them because it says so clearly what they feel and they want to show it to their partner. To people who describe a problem vividly and who end the letter saying they're too shy to see their doctors I often return their letter, and suggest, along with advice, that they should send a copy of it to their doctor because they've expressed their problem so well. And frequently it's much easier to write a letter to the doctor than to sit nervously in front of him trying to describe symptoms and anxieties that may suddenly sound absolutely ridiculous when faced with the great man himself.

Men, particularly, can often express themselves better in a letter than face to face, even to the ones they love. Examples of letters written from soldiers to their loved ones in times of war or from prison (the only times people seem to write letters these days) show how deeply emotions can be expressed on a page – emotions which, one suspects, might be difficult to say in words. A letter is communication, but without any of the accompanying risks of immediate confrontation.

My own feeling is that at least fifty per cent of the help that people get from writing to a problem page is simply from identifying the problem and writing it down. Fifteen per cent of the help is from actually getting a letter back, something which just says 'Yes, I hear what you say'; twenty per cent comes from any boost or compliment you can give them to make them like themselves more; and the final fifteen per cent is the actual advice.

The letter back also has some value as a thing in itself. A letter, unlike conversation, has a physical presence, like a present. Many is the time I've wailed to a friend about my problems and although the friend may have boosted me up loyally, their words only have a temporary effect. The next day I've either forgotten them or I've convinced myself I've imagined them. Or I feel sure they didn't mean them. But when these words are written down in a letter, I can never forget them. They're there for ever. Praise and compliments are some of the very special things that are so particularly nice about letters as opposed to conversation. Affectionate words which are spoken don't always last in our memory, particularly if our confidence is low; but when compliments are written down in a letter, they're there for ever. And that's why so many of us keep our old love-letters in the attic tied up with blue ribbon. It's so that when we feel very low we can crawl up the attic ladder, get them out, re-read them and think, 'Oh, well, at least someone once thought I was marvellous. I can't be that bad!'

Letters can be carried around; like totems, they can be touched.

I was moved to read Susan Hill's account, in her book, *Family* (Penguin, 1990), of how she wrote to the medical adviser on a woman's magazine when she was worried about conceiving. 'I had a reply which for months I kept close to me as a sort of talisman,' she wrote.

'I have it still. It reads:

"So that in spite of your recent unhappy obstetric history, and even while taking your age into account, I would encourage you most warmly to go ahead when you feel fit and ready, and conceive again, and would advise you that the odds are still strongly in favour of your succeeding and achieving a successful outcome to your pregnancy."

'It looked so good, so reassuring. I was so grateful to that unknown 'medical adviser' – I still am. It was a lesson to me, too, that writing to people like that, for advice and information, would produce more than a bald general or impersonal reply. There is a place for such people, the doctors on magazines and in the media, in much the same way as there is a place for Samaritans – to whom sometimes I have also turned for support and encouragement....'

I like the idea that Susan Hill still keeps that letter. It confirms my view that letters have a magic that words don't have. The letters I get are deeply personal expressions of strong emotions, and they prompt, in return, extremely personal and intimate advice, albeit from a stranger. There are no other letters that people ever get that are remotely like the ones that agony aunts send out. Bank managers do not send letters like ours; even friends and relations would prefer to say intimate things face to face than write them down.

So just getting a letter back is a physical expression of affection, even if it only consists of just a few brief, kind words. But of course most agony aunts don't write just a few brief, kind words. Our letters, at best, consist of four essential ingredients. And the first of those essentials is, of course, information.

This is an area that is dear to my heart – the spreading of information about clinics, groups, charitable organizations, societies, books, helpful tapes, helplines and so on. There is a plethora of these and yet so few people seem to know of them. I have around a hundred leaflets of my own, each of which lists many groups and books and tapes all related to specific topics. Added to this are some forty leaflets on similar subjects published by the Health Education Authority, Family Planning Clinics, drug companies, self-help groups and so on.

On the whole everyone knows about the big groups – Cruse, Brook, Relate and the Samaritans – but it's all those small energetic groups that I'm talking about, groups that are doing so much good and know far more about their individual subjects than I could ever know.

For instance, there is a lady at Faithfully Yours who will write to people who are unhappy because their pets have died; there is a group set up specifically to help young people tell their parents they are gay; a group for the siblings of the mentally handicapped, and groups for the children and families of alcoholics, happy to welcome even ancient relatives of alcoholics long since dead.

There are groups for violent men who wish to stop battering their wives, groups for men whose wives batter *them* and groups for parents whose children have committed suicide. There are associations for transvestites – and their wives – societies for those who are finding it difficult conceiving, or who are unhappy because they've had an abortion; there are agencies for people who want to find their natural parents, for ladies who want to find female friends to go on holiday with. There are self-help groups for gamblers, for people whose children have been abducted, for parents who have been wrongly accused of harming their children, for prisoners' wives and families, for people who have been accused of shoplifting, for people who want to know how to find a surrogate mother or who want to be able to make a dignified exit from life when they get too old.

There are groups for the innocent victims of crime – the friends and relatives of criminals who are often ostracized and blamed for the actions of their loved ones; there are groups for people with every medical condition under the sun – and for those who care for them; there's a helpline for people who are terrified of visiting the dentist, and groups for people frightened of flying; there are advisory services for people with special problems who want to go on holiday, for fathers who find access to their children difficult, for parents driven to distraction by their crying babies. And there are even two leaflets for people who have criminal records and want to know when and whether they have to declare them when applying for jobs. And hundreds more.

Where would most people find this information? Since so few people actually know that these organizations even exist, it's pointless to hope they will find their own way to them by asking at the library. And anyway, if you were an elderly person whose cat had just died and you were worrying about the wisdom of getting a new kitten in case it outlived you, I doubt whether your library or even your Citizens' Advice Bureau would know about the Cinnamon Trust which will help care for your pet if it outlives you. The only way these groups ever get known about is through local poster campaigns, through word of mouth – and through the feature pages and problem pages of newspapers and magazines.

When I arrived at *Woman* I was astonished to discover the wealth of help there is available that is completely hidden

from the general public unless members happen to get lucky
and stumble across an address here or there. Astonished and,
I must add, furious. There is a jealousy on the part of many
of the helping professions, a feeling that 'Too much
information is a bad thing and it's best if you don't know too
much about your condition which I shan't even name lest
you look it up in a medical dictionary and get the wrong end
of the stick because, being rather a simple-minded and stupid
person, you undoubtedly will.'

What woman has been told by her doctor, when she has a
miscarriage, of the Miscarriage Association? Or who has a
stillbirth, of the Stillbirth Association? Or the Hysterectomy
Association? Or if she's phobic, is she given the address of
the Phobic Action as well as given a referral to a
psychologist?

There are hundreds and hundreds and hundreds more of
these organizations, some good, some not so good, some
small, some big, some nationwide, some local – and an
agony aunt, as far as I know, is one of the very few people
who know about the existence of all these groups and is
prepared to hand it on.

My only gripe with the Samaritans is that, though
marvellous in many ways, they are extremely chary of giving
out addresses of groups – on principle. A friend who applied
to be a Samaritan was told, on the training course: 'Never
give an address or mention a group until the third call.'

The director of the Samaritans and I engage in friendly (I
hope) wrangles about the policy. 'Imagine', he once asked me,
'how extremely *un*supported someone would feel if they rang
the Samaritans with so much pain in their heart, asked for a
phone number as a tentative way of starting a conversation
and received it immediately. Oh well, goodbye then. Click.' he
once asked me. Very badly, I would think. But what about
getting sympathy, kindness, an address and another half hour
of listening and an invitation to call again please? To many a
helper, giving information seems to go hand in hand with

losing the patient or client. Or they see information as passing the buck, or a fobbing off. (It also, it has to be said, is extremely hard work to collect and keep up-to-date.) And yet information is really a treasure and a gift.

Dr Paul Hauck put this rather well in his book, *Hold Your Head up High* (Sheldon Press, 1991):

> When you receive counselling, what do you think is happening to you anyway? Aren't you learning about what causes emotional problems and how to avoid these painful conditions in the future? Of course you are. Well, if you know so much more than others, why not help them with all the interesting things you know? You'd pass on anything you learned in a first-aid class, wouldn't you? Would you not tell your children how to care for their teeth after a dentist instructed you? Surely you wouldn't keep that information to yourself merely because you weren't a dentist, would you? So get busy. Spread the word. If asked, educate.

I'm often asked whether I have, or rather who are, my 'team of experts'. I always love that question. I have visions of this row of wise men (almost certainly men) all with huge balding heads bursting with brains; they all wear glasses, of course, and round their white-coated shoulders hang large stethoscopes. In their hands are test-tubes and textbooks which they regularly consult; they sport long white beards, speak with Viennese accents and their fingers are permanently pinned together, in gestures of pompous assessment.

The truth is that of course I don't have a team of experts. *But I know where to find the experts if they're needed.* Often people write to us because the experts have failed them, but if they're in need of an expert, who better than an agony aunt to point them in the right direction? An expert would be useless to answer directly the problems that come in to me, anyway. No expert worth his or her salt would ever dream of diagnosing a medical problem on the basis of a letter alone and there's no greater help that I can give anyone than to tell them who to go to, or what book to read, or what society to join, to help them with their problem. I am proud to be a jack of all trades and master of none. I'm the person at the crossroads from whom you ask directions – and hopefully I point my enquirers the correct way (not forgetting to give them a hug and a few sandwiches to help them on their journey).

The second essential ingredient of a good reply is that it gives alternative views on a situation. I can look at it from different angles. I might be able to shake it out of the aspic in which it has become set and, by looking at it afresh, actually lessen its size. As an outside observer I can, if someone writes to me with the simple question like 'Shall I stay with my husband or run off with my lover?', point out that there are other options. For instance, she could try to improve her marriage; she could leave both of them and set up on her own; she could do nothing – an option which, as I remarked earlier, an awful lot of people never even consider as a positive solution.

Claire Rayner says: 'I try not to tell people what to do. I do tell people who are married to men who beat them up to, for God's sake, leave, but basically I try to give people strategies for coping, the skills to enable them to solve their own problems. I wish they'd teach it in schools.

'When people write in saying: "My problem is A and the only solution is X", you can often write back and say: "Well, actually I think your problem is not only A but B and C and the solutions available are not only X but Y and Z. Which one you choose depends on you. Here's a therapist, an organization, a leaflet with further information. Which you choose is up to you, too. Let me know how you get on." That in itself is enough. You're saying just by your reply: "I care, I think you're important." '

Irma Kurtz agrees. 'What I like about the job is the feeling of doing a jigsaw puzzle, putting the pieces together, thinking: she just hasn't thought of looking at it this way,' she says. 'Or maybe he can't help it. Or maybe he's not doing it to annoy her, maybe he's really miserable. Answering a problem should be like opening a cupboard and letting the light shine in. You just hope it gets through.'

More objective than someone close, I can, I hope, show readers the other sides to their question; I can point out that every marriage is in fact two marriages, seen from each partner's different viewpoint. It's often all too like the joke about the two Jewish mums who meet in the street:

> 'Well, Ruthie, and how are the kids?'
> 'To tell the truth, my Benny has married a slut. She doesn't get out of bed till eleven o'clock, she's out all day spending his money on God knows what and when he gets home exhausted, does she have a nice hot dinner waiting for him? No, she makes him take her out to a dinner at an expensive restaurant.'
> 'And Esther?'
> 'Ah, Esther. Esther has married a saint. He brings her her breakfast in bed, he gives her enough money to buy her all she needs and in the evening he takes her out to dinner at a smart restaurant.'

Has the writer thought about the situation from their partner's point of view? Have they actually told their partner how they feel? Lots of people write in who have never really expressed their gripes directly to their partners. They expect their partners to pick it all up through a kind of osmosis transmitted through banged doors and cold looks.

A third ingredient of help is advice. Directive advice is still a dirty phrase these days but there seems nothing wrong with it to me. I feel my readers would like to use me as they would a distant friend. And a friend always responds from the heart, saying what she or he thinks is the best. A bland letter back saying: 'Yes, I realize you are upset and I feel for you' isn't good enough.

Claire Rayner says: 'One of my jobs is to give people a pat on the back if they're doing well and a wallop a bit further down if they're not. It's quite legitimate to say, if you feel it, "That's a load of old codswallop." You can be opinionated and I am.'

Irma Kurtz says: 'My duty is simply to tell the truth. That is, in my case, the care and concern. The reason I'd hate to be a counsellor is because eventually you have to belong to a school or have a dogma and I'd hate that. I don't like being called a counsellor or a problem page adviser. Common sense is the best qualification. Also, we're always in danger of taking ourselves too seriously so I like the idea of being an agony aunt because it's rather light-hearted. It doesn't make us seem to have any system that always works. The best I can do is be a friend. We are a sort of family member, in a way. And that is another reason why I like being called an agony aunt.'

If a woman writes saying she is married to a man who regularly beats her and her children and puts her into hospital, what would her friend say? I'm saying nothing, it's up to you? I doubt it. She would be full of sympathy and back her up to the hilt in any plan to leave the man as soon as possible. Most of the letters I get cry out for advice and views and I think I'd not be fulfilling my role if I were merely to throw out loads of different options without adding which my recommendation would be. In the end it's always up to the reader what he or she does. It hardly needs to be stated again and again. Obviously there are moments when I can't really give any specific advice, but I can suggest questions they might ask themselves before reaching a decision, questions like: 'What is the right (and by right I mean moral) move to make – for me/ my children/ my partner/ my lover?', 'In the long-term is it kinder to say nothing to my alcoholic husband who is destroying his and my life and just stick faithfully beside him or would it be better for both of us in the long-term to issue an ultimatum?' (rather a loaded question that one, I'll admit!) and so on. While doing nothing is often quite a good answer, there are some situations where doing anything, just anything, is the only solution to break out of a particular deadlock.

'By doing nothing,' I remember one of my letter-answerers frequently writing, wisely, in her replies, 'you allow your partner to control the situation.' And of course, as Abraham Lincoln said, 'Silence is consent.'

Just as you cannot use ready-made answers to letters, there are no blanket rules in the giving of advice – it has to be tailor-made to the person who has written in. It's essential to keep an open mind. I always remember, long before I became an agony aunt, interviewing a then Marriage Guidance Counsellor and making the fatal mistake of referring to a 'normal' marriage. 'There is no such thing as a normal marriage!' the counsellor replied. And she illustrated this with an extraordinary story of an Irish woman she'd counselled that morning. Apparently her husband went out every single night, got completely drunk and never came home till the following morning when he would demand breakfast and a clean set of clothes.

When the counsellor, astonished, asked why she didn't leave this ghastly man, the woman replied: 'It's not the six nights out I mind. It's that he doesn't come home on the seventh!'

Apart from very basic laws like 'be honest, be kind, be loving', there just aren't any ground rules. Even the advice to 'talk your problems out' isn't always appropriate, either. It doesn't suit everyone. Personally I find that talking things out and discussing my feelings is useful in a relationship, but that's not to say there isn't a lot to be said, on occasions, for good old bottling things up. People who write in asking if they should tell their husbands about a drunken kiss and cuddle at the office party should, in my view, keep their traps shut. People who fantasize, while making love, that they're making love to Kevin Costner should do likewise. People who saw their best friend's husband kissing someone in a dark restaurant should also apply the Sellotape to their lips. And so on. Similarly with feelings. If every time your partner annoyed you to distraction, you protested, you would have no partnership left. Keep quiet (unless it persists) and it will pass.

Many men find that bottling things up is a good way of dealing with problems, and who's to say that sometimes it doesn't work best that way? If I *could* manage to deal with problems like that I'd certainly choose to because it's far less time-wasting and painful than all that recognizing and expressing. But I can't. I don't work like that. And whether it's because of how I am genetically, being female, or how I was brought up I don't either know or care. But I suspect that there *is* something genetic about it all. My own son, who was quite happy to cry when young (who has been around me, who cries at the drop of a hat, whose father never imposed any 'big boys don't cry' stuff on him), would rather die than be seen with red eyes by anyone. And indeed, for the last few years there have been very few red eyes to see. He has an extremely common-sense attitude to problems. But his: 'But, Mum, you can't do anything about it, why don't you just not worry about it until next week when you *can* actually do something about it? There's just no point in getting into a state' is met by my wailing: 'But I *am* in a state! I can't help it!' and my bursting into tears again. And it's usually only after lengthy discussions about the whole worry or anxiety with either a friend or my patient partner that I can get my act together and put the problem, if not to one side, at least somewhere where it doesn't get too much in the way.

Perhaps men have something to teach women in dealing with problems – just as much as women have to teach men. A sensible doctor (yes, they do exist in droves despite the impression you may have got so far from this book) recently wrote in a letter to the *Independent* that his experience was that you can always choose how to feel about a situation. 'When a few years ago my teenage daughter died suddenly of a brain haemorrhage,' he wrote, 'a bereavement counsellor was appalled that I hadn't gone through the normal gamut of emotions – disbelief, grief, anger and so on. She assumed I was suppressing these feelings. While I was certainly sad that my daughter had died and regarded it as most unfortunate, I never experienced the feeling or thought I should.... Preventing the feelings (that is, choosing not to have them) and suppressing the feelings (having them but not showing it) are two quite different things.'

There are no particular methods that work for everyone. It's horses for courses. The only views one can state categorically are moral views. And I think they should be stated. Don't hit children or demean them, do try to see the other person's point of view....

At this point even the Motherly Woman was starting to yawn so I jumped off my pulpit and asked for one of her delicious sandwiches.

And listen to Dr Ruth who was asked by a journalist why, if a woman wrote saying she was having an affair with a married man, she didn't say: 'Look you nasty cow, you are helping to break up a family. What you are doing is immoral and selfish. Find a man of your own and don't pinch someone else's.' The good doctor replied: 'I can't say *that* to somebody – my own morals and beliefs must never interfere with my therapy – maybe this woman's affair is the best thing that's ever happened to all three of them....'

Hmmph.

Apart from advice, agony aunts dispense sympathy. We deal in a vast range of human emotion. It seems to me that if you have experienced at least some of them, including pain and depression, you are better equipped to identify with others' pain. And it's interesting to find that so many agony aunts can easily pinpoint what it was in their childhood that made them turn into caring adults.

Claire, a great stoic and a believer in the words 'this too will pass' (which she uses to deal with the bad events in her life and the good) had an unspeakable childhood. Her father was a feckless good-for-nothing and her parents were both 'awful people ... barmy, potty, totally, utterly, hopelessly self-absorbed'. When she was wrongly put into a psychiatric hospital by them, at the age of sixteen, in Canada (she was in fact suffering from thyroid problems) no one visited her except once – her sister. And after she'd left Canada for sympathetic relatives in England who cared for her, she never saw either of her parents again – her choice. I always remember her saying, the first time I met her, 'Funny, do you know today I heard my father had died a month ago!' And when I said it was odd, she added: 'Yes, and only a month earlier I'd learnt my mother had died six months previously!' That is someone who did *not* have a happy childhood.

Deidre Sanders says: 'I get great satisfaction out of the job because I'm very nosy. I love knowing about people's private lives. I'm always bored by social chit-chat. But I love gossip, the dynamics of relationships, parents and children. I'll listen to anybody anywhere. Even on a train, if it's about their relationships I'll be there for the next three hours. It obviously satisfies something in me.

'This may have come from being troubled as a child, having had a difficult situation to cope with at home. I felt how awful it was that I and lots of other kids like me were carrying that unhappiness alone. I couldn't talk to anyone in the world about it. We shut our front doors and drew our net curtains and I never spoke about it to anyone, until I was perhaps twenty-one. It was mainly my mother, a very troubled person, who was trying to dull a lot of her problems with alcohol. I was caring for my mother instead of her caring for me, and it took me till the age of thirty-five to realize that was what I was doing. As far as I was concerned at the time, I was preserving my own life against the onslaught that she represented. I thought I'd come to terms with it all when she died when I was in my early twenties, but I hadn't. But I certainly came out of that believing that it is important, it is OK to talk about problems with people inside and outside the family.

'But I never want people to think I feel that I've got it all right either in my own life or in my replies. I try to remind myself every day that I'm a flawed human being. Complacency is a terrible trap.'

Angela Willans had a pretty horrific past, torn between a divorcing mother and father who used to pull her and her twin in different directions at railway stations while they argued about money. Angela's father was a gambler and many was the time the bailiffs came to the door and took the furniture away, leaving the twins sitting on packing cases. 'Then he'd go out and come back with a win, wanting to buy new furniture, not to pay off the debts he owed.' Angela and her sister both went to boarding school when they were seven years old – but before then had to suffer a nanny who used to torture them, both physically and verbally. She not only beat them with a hanger but she threatened them with the police, sometimes coming in several times a night to say that they were just about to arrive to take them away. The nanny's name was Olive, and Angela still cannot bear to eat an olive because of the associations.

'When I became an agony aunt I felt I'd come home, it was my niche. It's so rewarding, isn't it? People who have had a slightly unstable childhood have more of a need to be needed and this job fills that need. I feel that I can identify with the lost child in everyone.

'When I arrived at *Woman's Own* I went in for psychoanalysis because I thought some of the problems were so complex they needed more than I could offer. I thought: what makes us tick, why does this woman keep getting married to alcoholics, say? I felt sympathy but didn't understand, and my marriage was going through a bad patch and I began to feel, oh God I'm not making my husband happy, what's wrong with me, and it took psychoanalysis to make me see that no one makes anyone else happy. We do that ourselves. And it made me understand a lot about myself and therefore others. It's given me a lot. It's like a map of the workings of the human mind.'

Marje, however, had an extremely happy childhood, though her father, too, was a gambler. He ran pubs – five of them, one after the other – and as a result Marje went to eight different schools. 'He was a very funny man with a great sense of humour and mischief. He was also a great punter who used to disappear whenever he could to back horses and study form, and looking back I see what a life of anxiety my mother had.

'My interest first was in politics – an interest which sprang from witnessing the different types of customer in the saloon and public bar. I nagged my father from an early age to tell me why. And despite the fact that my father was a true blue Tory who would have loved Maggie, I became a socialist from the age of about five.

'The letters do depress me. Sometimes they make me cross but usually they depress me. I take quite a lot back home and often go to bed tossing and turning after reading them till the early hours. I have nightmares. Was it the right advice, what will happen if they do this or that? I react emotionally, yes. Unless you react emotionally to the letters, you shouldn't do the job.'

Her early 'training' for the job consisted of a crash course in How to Be an Advice Columnist, given her by her friend Dr Eustace Chesser, the sex psychologist. He coached her, over bowls of soup at lunchtime sessions, and taught her, she says, that 'a problem about a mother-in-law could indicate a sexual hang-up when you delved between the lines.'

Irma Kurtz also had a happy childhood. 'But from the beginning I've played a diplomat role. I've always tried slowly to change someone's life, to make someone see things a little differently. It's very difficult because the moment you pull them forward two inches they slide three inches back. Strangers always pick me on trains and buses. When I recently took a trip on a Greyhound Bus from Florida to California, I heard so many marital and emotional troubles from strangers on that bus. I think it's genuine curiosity. You have to be nosy and bossy to be an agony aunt.

'When I was quite young I remember elderly men would pick me up to talk about their problems. One picked me up when I was nineteen to have a soda in the middle of the day; he wasn't dangerous, he just wanted to talk to someone. In Manhattan!'

So even if you haven't experienced the pain of living in your past, you can still empathize with people's problems and give emotional advice. Evelyn Home was once asked (published in Evelyn Home Writes about Personal Problems 1970, IPC), 'How can you help people when you've never experienced their particular pain? Eg deserted wife, frustrated "other woman", rebellious son, sufferer from black depression?' She replied: 'I believe there are millions of injurious experiences but there are far fewer ways of feeling pain, mental or physical ... The pain of jealousy is the same as the pain of frustration. I've never been a condemned prisoner but I have waited in torment for a medical report which might have doomed me to permanent confinement in a wheelchair. All of us, I believe, feel pain to the limits of endurance during our lives – though the circumstances which produce it vary from person to person and we ourselves vary in our ability to react to it.' A Quaker, she did, actually, suffer from depression and still felt some weeks 'that I'd rather be dead, but I don't take my feeling seriously – it will pass'.

I feel everyone in the helping professions gets something out of helping others. I am sure that as we help others we help some damaged part of ourselves. When I was, at one point, struck with guilt at the pleasure I got from helping others, and the dependency I felt on other people's dependency on me, I mentioned these feelings to my GP, an exceptionally nice and caring woman. She gave me a scornful look. 'Of course you get something out of it. Why do you think I became a doctor?' she said. And Dr Paul Hauck says: 'Giving therapy is the same as receiving therapy. That's what I feel with practically everyone I counsel. We're both learning but I get it free.'

And John Bowlby, the psychologist whose research contributed so much to the theory of attachment between mother and child, has said that the craving for attachment suffered by the compulsive care-giver is satisfied by acting as a source of nurture rather than as the recipient. 'The person who develops in this way has found that the only affectional bond available is one in which he must always be the care giver, and that the only care he can ever receive is the care he gives.'

I was interested to hear Professor Anthony Clare, talking to Claire Rayner on a programme called *In the Psychiatrist's Chair*, saying that it was said of many doctors and many nurses that they actually have a lower threshold of pain than their patients – that they rush in because they can't bear the agony of empathizing with their clients. And Claire herself confessed that, when doing an essay on 'Is Nursing a Vocation?', she interviewed fellow-nurses who admitted that each of them was in nursing for some sort of ulterior motive. They all had a need that was being satisfied by the work they were doing.

'Since Proopsie [her husband] died, this job has become even more important to me,' admits Marje. 'There is nothing else in my life that really counts. When he died and I came back here after his death I felt this was like a second husband. But after all, I have been here for thirty-seven years. It's a bloody lifetime!

'I was interested to get a letter from a woman whose dog

had died after her husband had left her and her two teenage children had left home. She had adored this dog, it was her life, her company, her baby. She wrote in despair. One of the things she said was that she hadn't got anybody to care for. And as a result I had hundreds of letters from other readers, literally hundreds, never before had such a response. People have a great need to be needed.'

I see advice as a gift of love in itself. I'm often asked by people if I don't worry that my advice to people might not be wrong. Or, they ask, has anyone taken your advice and then come back to you saying it was the wrong advice? I try to be as polite as possible when asked these sort of inane questions, but underneath I always seethe. Because the question itself implies such a patronizing view of people and readers, as if they were such utter fools as to follow faithfully everything one wrote. People are never such chumps as to always follow anyone else's advice literally. But they often ask for it. And they're grateful for it. And if the advice they're given is offered with kindness and love, it merits being stored away in their minds along with all the other bits of advice until it comes out knitted into a plan of action they themselves have created. I don't for a moment think anyone getting a letter back from me is going to take my advice to the letter any more than I would take anyone else's advice to the letter. I would adapt and tailor it to fit me. Even if I asked a friend for advice about my future and she gave me the most ridiculous answer in the world, like: 'Why not give up your job and take up pottery in the country?' it would be useful. Because if nothing else it would make me think: 'Could I bear to give up my job? No. Would I prefer living in the country to the town? – No.' Her wild advice would have performed the function, if nothing else, of reaffirming how very happy I am in my job and in town.

I'm happy to say that the advice does, sometimes, seem to work. I don't get many letters of feedback, sadly – people only write in saying they wrote in once before and got good advice and now they're writing again – but now and again I'll get a touching card with a note saying how someone took my advice and things have worked out fine. One incident involved a girl who had written in about four times over the years about what to do with her farmer boyfriend with whom she was living but who refused to discuss marriage. She finally did take my advice to call his bluff. She packed her suitcase and walked out saying if he wasn't marrying her she was going. I was so pleased to get a letter from her saying, 'I did what you said at last! And guess what? I hadn't got half-way to the car with my suitcase when he came rushing up to me and proposed!'

What so few people realize is that you can threaten something like divorce if, say, your partner won't come with you to a Relate counsellor. This might well have the desired effect. But if it doesn't and you still want to stay married, then you don't have to go through with your threat. There again, you'll have gained some more information about your partner – that he'd rather you divorced him than accompany you for a few sessions with a counsellor. That of course might then make you rather more determined really to get a divorce!

The final ingredient for a successful, helpful letter is, of course, love, friendship and sympathy. Just the words 'I know you must be feeling terrible,' or 'I know in some small way how you feel because I have been through a similar experience myself,' are comforting to someone in misery and trouble. Just a line which conveys that you understand is a help in itself.

I never say: 'Pull yourself together,' and I never say: 'Think of all the people worse off than yourself.' When I printed a letter from a girl who was suicidal because her hair had been cut off I got lots of letters from people saying how trivial and why did I waste time on her when there were so many other people with so many other more important problems? But of course her problem was important, to her. The loss of her hair meant more than just hair – it must have symbolized the loss, perhaps of her sexual attraction, her femininity or, indeed, of control over her life. It's amazing how many women and even men feel fundamentally upset after a visit to the hairdresser.

And I always try to put in a compliment and give a boost to the writer's morale. If a mother writes saying she's yelling at her children, it's not going to help anyone if I tell her she's a bad mother and she must stop it. Her children will get shouted at worse than ever. But if I give that woman a little bit of a glow by saying that the fact she's written to me is a sign of her courage, the fact she knows there's a problem is a sign of her perceptiveness, the fact she's even written is a sign of how much she cares deep down for her children – all that, I hope, will make her have more confidence in herself and be less likely to shout at the kids.

I always remember the case of the student who shared a flat with a friend. His friend was lonely, couldn't get girlfriends and was becoming increasingly depressed. The student enlisted the help of three female colleagues and encouraged them to drop in and butter his friend up. They flirted with him, told him how attractive he was and generally boosted his morale. Within weeks he blossomed and got a girlfriend.

I think I learned the power of kindness after I'd got a letter from a woman who had an extremely complicated problem. Reading it through, it dawned on me in a flash that hers was a classic Freudian situation. She was clearly treating her husband as her father had treated her – and she regarded their daughter as a surrogate mother, taking out the resentment she felt for her grandmother on her sister-in-law – and so on. I forget the details but it all fitted neatly like a jigsaw puzzle. Feeling immensely proud of myself I brilliantly explained the situation to her as I saw it. But on reading it back I felt it was a trifle self-indulgent and cold, so: 'However, in conclusion, I must say that you sound to me the most super person,' I added, as a warm afterthought. 'You have suffered your problems so bravely, you've been a terrific wife and a wonderful mother and you come across as such a nice, courageous person. You really do deserve a break.' I had a letter back from her by return. She had, rightly now that I look back on it, virtually ignored all my analytic meanderings.

'Dear Virginia,' she wrote, 'I can't tell you what your letter meant to me. No one has ever called me brave or courageous or a good mother ever before. I keep your letter in my bag and when I feel low I get it out and read it and I cheer up at once.'

Another typical response came from a different reader: 'Dear Virginia, back in November I received your reply to what must have been a very sad letter indeed. I thank you sincerely for your praise, compliments and appreciation. You described me as a "very special person". I had never thought of myself as that, only different ... I showed your letter to my shrink and he was quite impressed, despite his mumblings about "standard letters" etc, etc. Your letter helped at the time. No matter how insincere he thought it was! I believed it and that's what mattered. Thanks again! Lotsa love ...'

'Paul' wrote: 'The first step was writing this letter. The second will be posting it. The third will be your reading it whoever you are. I'll probably never meet you but you will know forever a part of my life that no one else apart from myself knows about. I hope you understand why I need to do this and all I can say is that I'm deeply indebted to you.'

Reading this, you may wonder how I remember these personal replies that have come in (and there are many others). I never printed them on the page. I remember them *because I've kept them*. Like the people I write to, who keep my letters, I too, cherish complimentary letters from strangers. When I read them back, I get a warm glow. Which just shows how powerful a letter can be.

*   *   *   *

The party is starting to thin out. The Computer Programmer makes his excuses and looks forward, he says, to hearing from me. I am thinking of leaving myself when I hear an encouraging wailing from a room upstairs. The baby has woken up. I'll get a glimpse at last. And a chance to give him his teddy. I pour a final drink and wander across to the Neighbour – but as I approach, she turns to rush upstairs to her son. Of course, it could have been just that she saw me coming and ran....

'Aha! The agony aunt!' says the Blazer triumphantly behind my back. 'I was just talking about you to my friend here.'

A rather gloomy make-upless girl with greasy hair smiles a wan hello. I feel that she is either a librarian or a social worker. She turns out to be the latter. 'Agony aunt,' she says, as if the words were lemons in her mouth. She gives a kind of patronizing sneer as if I were Mrs Thatcher, The Sun *and Dr Rhodes Boyson all rolled into one.*

'She does much the same job as you,' says the Blazer, rather puzzled that I am getting the cold shoulder.

'I hardly think so.'

'Not at all like you,' I say, greasily. 'You do marvellous work.'

'And so do you,' said the Blazer, loyally. I am coming round to him.

'I suppose,' says the Social Worker, reluctantly, 'that you do manage to dispense quite a lot of useful information. But it's always so obvious that all the letters are invented.'

'Invented?' I cry. 'Invented?' The Neighbour looks startled as she comes through the door carrying her howling baby. 'You must be joking!'

'Of Course They're All Invented ...'

When any market research is done on a magazine or newspaper that carries a problem page, it's always discovered that the agony column is one of the most highly-read pages in the publication. Surveys done on some magazines shows that the problem pages are usually read by a staggering ninety per cent of readers. And invariably it's the second or third most popular feature (or furniture, as regular columns like ours are called), making up a popular three-piece suite along with the horoscopes and the medical pages. Why are so many readers drawn to it?

Lots of people read them in order to get reassurance that there are people worse off than themselves. In other words, things may be bad, but they're nothing like as bad as for the people who write in to the agony column. 'The recognition factor is one of the biggest reasons why people read the page,' says Claire Rayner. 'I remember a taxi-driver once refusing to take my fare because he said: "I read your column and you've helped me a lot." And yet he'd never even written to me.'

Many people must read it for the information that's offered that they can't get anywhere else.

'Various organizations which could no more pay for advertising than fly to the moon have depended on us,' says Claire. 'Relate is a case in point. Never had to take an advertisement. They had us. Indeed none of the self-help groups have ever taken paid advertising but we've always provided it, and rightly so.

'And people read the column for basic sex education.
That's where I first got my own – sure as hell no one ever told
me anything.'

And loads of people read it in the way that people like
reading other people's diaries even though they know they
shouldn't. Snooping is great fun. And the page *is* a
fascinating snoop, as riveting as the muffled comments and
sobs heard through a crack in the doctor's surgery door. No
one can deny, either, that lots of people read the page for a
laugh, as well.

'Certainly lots of people read the page out of voyeurism.
There's no harm in that,' says Claire.

But my own feeling is that most people read it for its
healing qualities. I like to see the page as a kind of
mini-symphony, full of small minor tunes that are resolved
with major cadences. Each problem is a cry; each answer is a
hug. Everyone loves reading happy endings and the pleasure
got from reading a problem page is a bit like the pleasure got
from seeing a lost, crying child in a supermarket suddenly
run to her mum who's found her at last.

All editors recognize the appeal of this syndrome. At
Woman the features editor would regularly produce
something from her file of what were referred to as TOTS –
Triumphs Over Tragedy Stories. These would be 'heart-
warming' stories – like that of the boy found in the Brazilian
jungle, given a new face by a Scottish surgeon who eventually
adopted him, or Evelyne Glennie, the deaf drummer. All
interviews with stars that run on the lines of 'My life was
wrecked by drink and drugs until I met my wife/found the
Lord/took up yoga' are just large versions of problem letters.
Even the more upmarket papers feature their own versions of
TOTS, like the extracts of William Styron's book on his own
depression in the *Independent*.

The problem page supplies these TOTS in miniature – only
on the page the readers provide the tragedy and the agony

aunt provides the (potential) triumph.

As I've said, I've always thought that answering people's problems is rather like lighting a fire for a freezing man. As the fire burns, some of the warmth inevitably comes your way. But even if you're just a passing bystander witnessing the scene you can still feel the heat of the flames. It's a nice feeling which really does 'warm the heart'.

The job of editing the page is quite a different one from the huge task of answering readers' letters. Indeed, to most agony aunts, the page itself is just the tip of the iceberg. But like all tips of icebergs, it's an important and crucial part of the work. I happily jabber on about helping and heart-warming but no one employs me because I'm a nice person. I'm employed as a journalist to write a good, readable page. I'm employed for my writing and editorial skills rather than for my caring and compassion. Magazines and newspapers have to be sold. And all agony aunts agree that they are writers first and foremost.

Claire makes seventy-five per cent of her income from books. Angela sees herself as a writer first, and is now working on her fifth book. Irma has written many books and is working on her second novel. This book is my tenth. Deidre Sanders thinks herself as primarily a journalist. 'I used to make a newspaper for cats when I was eight years old. It was called *Miaow Weekly*, and the eye for detail was astonishing, I got all the furniture of a newspaper, the weather, fashion, letters, even a problem page. I'm amazed when I look at it now.

'And an ability to write is crucially important. Perhaps if you look at me and my time, producing the page is ten per cent of the work. But I'm always conscious of the fact that the column has to be right and readable. I know when it's seen at the paper it's always judged as fresh copy. It has to be a gripping read. I don't dispute that. I say it's right and necessary. You can't have an unreadable column. The column is a signpost to the other service.'

And Marje, author of two books, goes further. 'Although none of the letters on the page are made up, they make me feel like a fiction writer. They build up as a story in my mind when I'm working on them. I can see the people sometimes and so I'm writing like I might write something for television, a script, say.'

So how is the page compiled?

First of all I've got to set the record straight about the question 'Don't you just invent all the letters?' The answer is always, 'No – but if only it were necessary!' Sadly there are enough extraordinary, sad and astonishing letters that come to my office every day to fill the page ten times over each week.

I'm often asked, too, if the problem page is representative of my postbag. The answer is – not completely. If the column were completely representative it would be largely an unreadable collection of depressed and lonely people, week after week. But if the column were simply made up of the bizarre, saucy and kinky letters that come in, it wouldn't be remotely representative. The trick is to get a balance between the two. First there has to be a lead – a letter that is slightly more important than the rest. Sometimes it will be a shocking one, perhaps from someone who has suffered from child abuse or violence. Or perhaps it will be one on a subject that everyone can identify with that is particularly well written. I'm always so grateful to the writers who express themselves well, because I know their letters will touch a chord in the readers. Many is the reader who has written in to me saying that they can't sleep for mulling over some act of cruelty they've read about on the page. Or: 'That lonely man's plea touched me so much I can't stop thinking of him, please can we get in touch?' Or even: 'I was so moved by the unhappiness of the young girl who wrote. I'm the mother of two very happy teenagers and we feel we're so very lucky. I would love to correspond with this girl if you could put us in touch.' The page definitely needs letters that inspire response.

Then I usually try to get in a bit of hard information – an address, a book, a group. When I mentioned a group called Self-Help in Pain, which helps people with chronic pain problems like arthritis or injury, they got a thousand enquiries. The Asthma Society, when I mentioned it, received five thousand. A book I mentioned about irritable bowel syndrome sold a thousand mail-order copies.

I also like to have a little regular spot on the page which links readers from week to week. At *Woman* I used to have The Other Half, the special spot for men. I felt that otherwise the page could so easily become a dreadful whine from women about men. I also thought it would be useful for women to have the male point of view, to remind them that men had problems too, problems with love and feelings. We also tried out a spot called Good News, in which readers were encouraged to write in with uplifting experiences, examples of how they'd overcome some intolerable problem. Unfortunately I got so many letters from people who had found Jesus and so few from people with perhaps more practical solutions that we dropped it in the end. At the *Sunday Mirror* I published a selection over the months called 'Words of Wisdom' – little phrases and poems that people had found helpful. I know it sounds dreadfully sentimental but for me these are sheer rock and roll and I come out in goose-pimples whenever one hits the spot. I enjoyed that spot just as much as the readers, and my secretary and I were regularly getting tears in our eyes at contributions.

I mean, who can resist 'If fate throws a knife at you there are two ways to catch it – by the blade or by the handle'? Or 'It only takes two muscles to smile but twenty-two to frown. Why waste all that energy?'

I'd come in all snapping from some slight or piece of nonsense that I imagined (or didn't imagine) I'd suffered from the features department, wanting to kill everyone on sight and I'd then read something like:

Don't look for the flaws as you go through life,
And even when you find them,
It is wise and kind to be somewhat blind,
And look for the virtue behind them.

And then, dammit, I'd find myself bursting with love and affection for the entire wonderful human race. Sickening.

This series 'Words of Wisdom' was followed by up by a collection of poems for bereaved people – more tearjerkers. It got to the point when, sniffing, I'd throw the latest hit to my secretary to read and she'd sniff back that she couldn't take any more, they were all too moving.

Now each week I have a topic I discuss like phobias or alcoholism, with suggestions of further help. And each week I also feature nine of a bank of seventy phone help-lines on various topics of interest to readers. These 0898 numbers are a sore point with most people. The fact is that they are hideously expensive, particularly during peak telephoning times. I wish they were cheaper – but I do know that most of the calls are either made on Sunday or in office hours during the week. I also know, from the number of people who ring these lines, what an absolute boon they are to people with problems, people who may not have the oomph to go to a library and start riffling through the files for information on the subject.

It's nice to have a sexy letter on the page now and again. At *Woman* I was always being begged by various editors to put more sexy letters in, but funnily enough at the time of writing no one's ever mentioned it to me. What's amused me is that, from being the one who wrote all the saucy things in *Woman* magazine and seeing myself as a rather daring contributor to a world of recipes and knitting patterns when I talked about penises and orgasms, the situation at the *Sunday Mirror* has so far been completely reversed. In comparison to some of the rest of the paper, the page often reads like 'Thought for the Day'. I turn the pages which feature stories about judges who dress up as women and television personalities who go with call girls and reach my page where I find I am sitting, like some dour Scottish minister, proclaiming that it is wrong to have affairs when you are married, wrong to treat your children badly, wrong to ... you name it and I've usually got a pretty stuffy answer to it.

I'm often asked about editors' reactions to my answers and whether they like to put an oar in now and again. I've always found they're too busy to worry about the answers, and they only interfere if they happen to read the column and something strikes a real emotional chord with them. When I wrote in an answer to a parent who was furious that her son was homosexual, I said that the boy couldn't help it and most homosexuals would much prefer to have been born straight as it would make life so much easier. I got a message that the then editor had declared this to be 'Not true!' We all looked at him rather differently after that.

Another editor claimed that my answer to a woman who complained that her husband rang his elderly and lonely mum for a quick chat every night was wrong. I'd said that it sounded as if she was married to a really nice man and what was wrong with ringing his mum every night? The editor thought it was most peculiar and we agreed to differ by taking the letter out completely. I've always wondered, however, what was the relationship she had with her own mother. Vairy eenterestink, I seenk, as Freud might have said.

There were probably more editorial oars put in in the past when it was thought inappropriate to mention certain words. In the early days of Evelyn Home, she couldn't use the word 'masturbation'. It had to be described as a 'particular habit'. 'Sexual intercourse' was referred to as intimacy (in her autobiography Evelyn Home remarked that one reader referred to being 'intermate' with her partner, which she felt was a particularly apt and nice way of putting it).

For a while she could not use the word 'bottom', not even 'bottom' of the garden or 'bottom' of a saucepan.

Agony aunts today can suffer the reverse. 'I've been nagged for more sex letters,' says Claire. 'Once I said, "Well, sweetie, if the letters come in, fine." So my editor said she'd like to see the original letters. From then on I always sent the original letter attached to the copy so they always knew they were real letters.

'I censored myself sometimes,' she adds. 'In the very early days I would never publish a letter about incest. But I worked gradually. Eventually I managed to get in a letter about an uncle and a niece. The editors could handle that better than a father and a daughter!

'There were things that I knew I wouldn't get past them. I never went for the "Ooh! Fancy that!" factor. I always wanted the breath of recognition from the reader. But of course I got such numbers of letters from readers on some subjects that it was impossible not to mention some subjects eventually. I had trouble with the editors over homosexuality for a long time, but eventually it got onto the page. And I always had more problems with letters about lesbians than letters about gay men. I think that reflected some of the male attitudes on the paper.'

There was an alarming quote in *Stick It Up Your Punter: The Rise and Fall of the Sun* by Peter Chippindale and Chris Horrie (Heinemann, 1990). 'Another click might take him [Kelvin MacKenzie, editor of the *Sun*] to the "Dear Deidre" agony-aunt column. "What's she going on about today?" the muttering would continue as he screwed his eyes to read the column. "Fuck it," he would mumble, raising his voice as he issued another instruction. "This stuff's useless. Get something a bit dirty in here, will you? Tell her to put a dirty letter in here, eh? The readers don't want this crap." ' And even Nathanael West's Miss Lonelyhearts suffered from the dreadful editor, Shrike. 'Once he had tried to get fired by recommending suicide in his column. All that Shrike had said was: "Remember, please, that your job is to increase the circulation of our paper. Suicide, it is only reasonable to think, must defeat this purpose." '

And Angela Willans has been on the receiving end of both sorts of editors. 'Under one I felt there was some censorship – it was in the eighties and there was a definite feeling against mentioning lesbianism or homosexuality, but it crept back in. There've been times the language has changed. In the seventies you could talk about penises and penetration but not penetration and a vibrator. They wanted more about sex, but without the words. They wanted titillating sexual letters, not straightforward ones. I remember one editor saying: "Oh, yes, I like premature ejaculation!"

'I've always thought of the private letters as the real job and the page as the shop window. I've always tried to choose letters for the page that will appeal to a vast number of people. I want people to open up about that problem. When I wrote about a daughter who hated her mother, masses of people wrote in sympathizing because they realized that they weren't alone. They were the same. There was nothing wrong in it. And I had not judged the girl who wrote in. I'd accepted it.'

The final problem with the page can be the sub-editors. The only trouble I had was when one changed the sentence that read: 'Transvestites are usually not homosexual' to 'Transvestites are usually homosexual.' She just couldn't believe the truth. And when Claire was working on a newspaper in the early days she was infuriated when a sub altered her copy. 'I had a letter from a mum who had found her children playing doctors and nurses behind the sofa with their pants and knickers down. That wasn't the problem but it appeared on the page as "with their clothing disarranged". I was so angry I thought I'd get my own back and it took me three months. A man had written in about his wife who never felt like sex in the morning when he was keen, but was always ready for it at night, when he was zonked out. You know – larks and owls. So I wrote in my answer: "Some men are constitutional early risers ..." and it got in. No one noticed it, no one wrote. But *I* knew I'd done it. I'd got my own back and it cheered me up no end.'

'The problem with subbing,' says Irma, 'is that it has to be done so carefully. When a girl writes to me about her problem I am actually answering her, and the advice that I give her may not be what I would give a person who phrased a similar problem slightly differently. If the phrasing is subbed out, my answer can be inappropriate.'

The only time anyone usually wants me to take a letter out is if it's appeared in someone else's column.

Some sensible readers don't just write a letter and bung it off to one agony aunt. They write a letter, photostat it several times, and bung it off to a variety of agony aunts. The result, since we can all spot a good letter a mile off, is that if we're not careful we quite often find ourselves printing the same letter. Claire and I recently each printed a letter from a woman who wanted to kill her husband by either plunging a knife into his throat or poisoning his shepherd's pie. (Claire advised that the wife encourage her husband to get help for his depression from the family doctor; rather unsympathetically perhaps, I recommended divorce.) Barbara Jackson of the *Sunday People* and I often get the same letters. Even more interestingly, we often make the same kinds of alterations to stop the readers being recognized.

I recently had a letter from a chap which ran: 'A goodlooking single man has just moved in next door. I go to work every day and have let myself go rather to seed. When I returned early one day I found my wife and this neighbour on our bed upstairs. They were fully clothed and said they were just testing the springs. I know it sounds ridiculous, but could they have been just testing the springs? We got the mattress only recently and both my wife and I have been complaining that it wasn't a good buy.' This is an obvious letter for the page. But it was such a good letter, in fact, that I noticed that Deidre Sanders had printed it as well. I wondered how many other agony aunts had got the mattress-springs letter, and, talking to Marje found that she had also received it. But, perhaps wisely, she suspected it was a hoax and had refused to print it. This letter is what my editor at *Woman*, Jane Reed, used to call an 'Oooh, Maureen!' letter. She insisted that there must be at least one letter that would make whoever was reading the page suddenly nudge her friend (in this case Maureen) and exclaim 'Oooh, Maureen!' to her. (On the *Sun*, apparently, this is known as the 'Hey, Doris!' factor.)

One of the reasons people so often suspect the letters on the page of being invented is that they can't believe they all arrive in neatly-packaged 200-word paragraphs. They're right there. Letters have to be edited, and frequently severely. After all, they come in sometimes ten or twenty pages long; they have to be cut. Often one single problem has to be removed from a host of others for scrutiny; but letters also have to be re-written, often, to make the readers' families unable to identify them. Most agony aunts will print any letter that doesn't have the words 'Please do not print' on it – and even then if a problem's particularly good she'll often write back to the reader enclosing a much disguised and edited version asking permission to use it. Often she gets a positive reply. But no agony aunt ever likes the idea of people who write in recognizing themselves, only their problems. Although everyone who writes in must realize that there's a chance their letter will be printed, if you're upset and anxious you sometimes forget to write 'Please don't print' at the top. Or maybe you think you don't mind at the time but if you saw all the details paraded over Sunday breakfast you'd realize you'd made a big mistake. So a letter from a woman who works in a bank, has three children, and lives in the north of England may become a woman who works in a shoe-shop, has two children and lives in the south. And I remember a man who wrote in having lost his sporting confidence when elected leader of his local darts team, who became, on the page, the leader of his local bowls team (or was it the other way round?)

I learnt to disguise letters early on when I printed a letter from a lady in the north of England who was getting fed up with her aunt who kept getting her to come round to change the lightbulbs and so on. There were other details printed that made her instantly recognizable. I got a horrified letter back from the reader, who had been scouring Cumbria for copies of *Woman* to keep her aunt from seeing them. Had I changed the details there would have been no problem at all. (After that episode, by the way, we became pen-friends and correspond to this day.)

One woman wrote in with a problem that I disguised so thoroughly she didn't even realize it was her. I got a letter from her saying: 'You probably don't remember me but I wrote to you recently and got a nice reply. Last week you had a letter from someone and it sounded as if she had a very similar problem. Would it be possible to forward the enclosed letter to her so that we can get in touch?' I took the easy way out and said that she hadn't given her address.

I'm not saying accidents don't happen. About twice I've printed a letter that has upset the reader who either didn't realize, or realized too late, that the letter would appear on the page. Luckily there were no repercussions in their families beyond their own understandably hurt and furious feelings.

Perhaps the worst mistake I ever made was in printing the wrong number for Gay Switchboard.

When it dawned on me what I had done I practically had a heart attack. I'd only recently seen an end-of-year report for Gay Switchboard and it featured one of those cakes split up into slices showing what proportion of calls were what. A high proportion that year were hoax calls. This made matters even worse. I could imagine a furious woman being hauled up in the middle of the night to answer the phone only to find giggling voices down the other end shouting 'Pooftah!' at her. Taking my courage in my hands I rang the number I'd put on the page. No answer. The phone rang and rang and finally it was picked up by a weary little man who had obviously come a long way to answer the phone. In my mind I could hear his carpet-slippers along the worn linoleum of his corridor, hear his painful cough; I could see his shabby dressing gown, his grey hair, bandaged leg ... my God, his walking frame!

I gabbled out my apologies in hysteria, feeling like an absolute shit not to have checked the number first and to have prevented the misery the poor guy must have gone through. At the end of my squirming burble of grovelling there was a slight pause. Then a thin voice spoke. 'Not to worry, dear,' he said, kindly. 'I know, these things happen. There have been a few calls and they have been a bit inconvenient but that's life. Bye, bye, dear.'

Having envisaged IPC being sued for damages having caused some elderly woman to have a nervous breakdown and me being sacked and not being able to pay the mortgage and having to pay damages myself for the rest of my life, handed on to my son ... you know the tricks your mind plays ... I was so relieved I felt like ringing him up again to ask his address so that I could send him a bottle of champagne. Or six bottles of champagne. I was about to dial when I thought better of it. Who was I to bring him yet again to the phone? He'd had enough bother already.

The page can actually help people directly. Deidre Sanders of the *Sun* received an anonymous letter from a woman who'd made thirteen suicide attempts saying she was going to kill herself and take the children with her. She'd had very bad post-natal depression and her husband had been involved in a near-fatal car crash just before she gave birth so she had to give birth not knowing whether he was dead or alive. He did actually survive. 'Whereas normally I would disguise people as much as possible before putting something like this on the page, in this case I ran it in the paper and ran every specific detail which was there. I wanted her family to know it was her. And as a direct result she was taken into a mental hospital so she could receive treatment and that the children would be safe. A friend let us know where she'd been admitted and now I'm writing to her. We are maintaining contact with her. *I'm* actually writing to *her*, not waiting for her to write to me, and I just hope it helps.'

Another time Deidre's column saved the day was when she got an anonymous letter from a single parent. She loved her seven-week old baby but couldn't cope. She kept going out and leaving the baby. She didn't give it much to eat. She thought it was dying. 'I put her letter in the column, plus the telephone number of Parents Anonymous and hoped she'd contact them. We waited all day, very keyed up. And at five in the afternoon she rang them. They paid her train fare to come over and arranged for her and the baby to go into hospital where the baby was found to be surprisingly well but the mother was suffering from the most terrible post-natal depression. What I wasn't prepared for was the fact that on that day Parents Anonymous heard from over fifty mothers, some in a much worse state than the girl – mothers who'd seen the number in the paper. One mother had half-strangled her ten-year-old son.'

So not only can the page help directly, but it can give people confidence to realize they're not alone. Would those mothers have rung the number if it had just been given on its own? There must have been something about reading about that girl and seeing that if someone was, it seemed, starving their baby to death and not being condemned by Deidre – indeed being recommended to ring a number for help – then why couldn't they do the same? Obviously, Parents Anonymous wouldn't condemn this girl if she rang, according to Deidre, so presumably they wouldn't sit in judgement on them, either.

So many people get help just by reading of the other silly things people worry about, and often from reading about a problem they'd never dare confide in anyone else on the page.

I once had a letter in from a woman of thirty-one who still sucked her thumb. Was she normal, she asked. I wrote back that she was just as normal as anyone who smoked cigarettes or bit their nails (I still bite my nails at forty-seven), and was amazed to get a flood of letters from other middle-aged women who still sucked their thumbs – 'particularly while watching telly'!

As far as the answers on the page go, I do like to put something of myself in. It's terribly easy to slip into a kind of auto-pilot mode, churning out sentences with words and phrases one would never use in real life, like 'It really is important that you discuss this with your partner', 'I suggest you seek counselling', 'I was saddened to hear of your recent loss'. Many's the time I go back over a recent column before it's printed and weed out these beastly phrases like a mine-sweeper and try to make the tone more personal. It's particularly important because readers like to know that agony aunts, too, can suffer just as many irrational, inane problems as they themselves. As one who feels daunted and miserable when I come across someone who seems to 'know all the answers' – and prefers to seek help (whoops, there I go again) from people who can tell me how they felt the same and how they overcame it – I'm sure my readers feel the same about the page. The only problem has been when an editor has insisted I take out some confession I've made on the grounds presumably, that their agony aunt should be above reproach and eminently sane and sensible. '*Three* abortions, Virginia? Surely not! I think you should keep that to yourself!'

Well, it depends on what sort of agony aunt you want. If you want someone who preaches to you from above, who tells you what to do without explanations, who's like the doctor you approach with a problem who silently writes you out a magic prescription while saying nothing about it – and there are many who really do find this approach suits them – then all well and good. Evelyn Home started her habit of adding 'my dear' to her answers, for instance, in order to make her seem more mature when she was in her twenties. Personally, however, I prefer someone who talks to me on equal terms, someone to reassure me by telling that they, too, have felt as silly or mad as I do; and then telling me how they coped with it.

When suffering post-natal depression after the birth of my son, and finding myself imagining harming him and his friends by torturing them to death in the most repulsive ways – fantasies that tormented me horribly – I didn't want to see someone who would just tell me not to worry, or suggest I saw my doctor. I wanted to meet someone – and preferably someone sane, normal and responsible – who'd say: 'I had exactly the same! It's frightful! But it'll go away!'

The more you can put yourself over in the column as a real person, someone, in my case, who's been divorced, been a single parent, got a child, spends half her time cooking and washing and worrying, the more like a friend you become. My features editor at the *Sunday Mirror* claims that he knows all about my private life since he went down to the cuttings library and read my columns from day one.

What I do find odd is how often I get letters from people who seem to suffer the same problems as I do. I got a letter from a woman who wrote in saying that two months after his grannie had died, her twelve-year-old son had suddenly become obsessed with her death and death in general. He was in tears at the weekend, certain he was going mad, and was sure the end of the world would come and everyone would be dead. He was always ringing up in tears from school, and so on. Astonishingly, my son had only just come through a similar experience and was petrified of the idea of nuclear war, and I was extremely keen to put this lady's letter on the page. I asked my son if he would mind my mentioning that he had suffered the same experience as this boy and he said not at all if it would help anyone else in the same situation. I wanted her to know that my son simply got over it in a matter of time. Separation anxiety (for this is what it is) is a common problem among children of that age as they start to grow up and realize that one day they will have to be separated from their parents.

When this kind of coincidence occurs I'm often reluctant to put the letter in the column because I'm sure my friends would think I'd invented it. A similar coincidence occurred during the Gulf War when I really wanted to get something on the page about mothers of teenage boys and their worries that they might be called up. This was a worry of my own, though everyone told me I was being completely mad. Luckily a woman wrote in with exactly that problem, though her sons were twelve and twenty, so I was able to ring up our political correspondent 'on behalf of a reader' to find out the facts.

(I have, in fact, been known to find out quite a bit 'on behalf of a reader' when I have problems of my own. I feel a bit like those people who went to see Sherlock Holmes to ask about a friend in a fix. I'm always waiting for the lady at the end of the phone to say: 'My dear Miss Ironside. I think from the timbre of your voice, your distinctive vocabulary, the fact that I detect a slight sore throat, that there is no "reader". You are asking, if I am not mistaken, on behalf of none other than yourself!' Whereupon I will collapse into a guilty heap.)

I don't often get criticism of the page. But readers do pick me up on the odd word. 'How dare you always refer to doctors as "he"!' (They are, mostly.) 'How dare you refer to mental hospitals!' (This was when I'd suggested that someone try to let the horrible remarks of her neighbour wash over her by imagining that, as the neighbour looked out of her window, a large sign appeared above her front door in golden letters saying 'Mental Hospital'. Thank God I hadn't said loony-bin.) 'How dare you refer to the adopted child's mother as her "real mother"!' ('Birth mother' is the expression.) 'How dare you refer to someone as a half-caste!'

(Mixed race is correct.) 'How dare you refer to an AIDS victim!' (There is no such thing as an AIDS victim in AIDS-speak. Sufferers – or perhaps that's not the correct word – are 'people living with AIDS'. AIDS is a minefield of political jargon, by the way. Or do I mean HIV? And do you contract it or do you catch it? Whatever you do, you never suggest that it's prevalent in Africa because that's racist.) 'How dare you refer to do-gooding vicars' wives!' This from a canon. I'd referred to the do-gooding vicars' wives by saying that Relate counsellors were trained and not DGVWs, and got back a justifiably angry letter from the canon who was married to a woman who, according to him, did nothing but help battered wives, raped teenagers (helped them, that is, not raped them), Indian girls possessed by devils and so on. I was suitably chastened.

Obviously all agony aunts get their fair share of letters from Disgusted of Tunbridge Wells. This one says it all – it was written on one of those old typewriters that ate out the holes of the 'o's.

It so happens that I visit a launderette nearby once a week and it is there that I invariably find some of your publications, some old, many quite new.

On this occasion, which happened to be last Tuesday, I found a copy of your magazine lying on one of the small tables. Apparently it had been read and left as the buyer apparently might have found the contents uninteresting.

As a rule I at no time can afford to keep putting out 20p a time, sometimes more, to read such magazines. I find nothing very novel and interesting in them, yet on an unexpected chance do I come across an item on which further development can be made. But I do like to scan the marvellous letters people of both sex send in for intended publication, and it is on this theme and evidence that I have cut out the attached. [This was a letter about a woman asking if it was dangerous for her husband to suck her breasts during intercourse.] When I read such letters, the first thing that comes to mind is to assess the type of person who might be responsible for sending your firm such letters. To my mind, most letters refer to sexual acts and activities. There is also a vast majority that are sent in from those outside the marriage boundaries and there are many who have no idea of what is known as the 'Sanctity of Marriage'.

Apart from anything else, I often wonder what young people's reaction is to this trash as I call it, and yet how harmful can it lead to? (*sic*)

I do know that ignorance plays a very important part when the innermost feeling and actions are made manifest through a paper or magazine and added to this, I must admire the conjured-up retorts that are also published as replies to each incident. [I think here she is implying that my *replies* are invented. A new twist on an old theme.]

Britain proclaims its Christianity usually around Christmas and forgets about it a week after. Yet in any manner of Christian spirit, how can anyone divulge the innermost secrets of a married bed chamber for the world to gawk and criticize? There must definitely be something very wrong and unnaturally maintained.

Shallow-mindedness invariably expresses itself the way letters of this calibre go, of this there is no doubt whatsoever ...

I would also say that if one is to credit the way this article is expressed, I would naturally assume that the individuals concerned are living lower than animals and resemble what takes place when a bitch is on heat and the male does his rituals before the final job?

It's a shame the country has sunk to this and that such letters and literature is allowed to float out to so many thousands in a corrupt and impure atmosphere.

I hope those responsible will realize that one day before the judgement seat, all of this will have to be declared and accounted for?

Please don't reply to me direct it would be better that your retort to my letter be published in your next issue. Maybe when I go to the launderette next, a copy might be left for others to read and that some sort of explanation is rendered on the basis as to why such letters are ever sent in at all?

Right on! I didn't like the lady's comments, but I liked her style – which is why I kept the letter.

Irma Kurtz gets especially abusive letters from the States. 'Particularly if I've written about having an abortion. At Christmas I get Christmas cards saying: "Merry Christmas, mummy, from your unborn baby", with dreadful pictures of foetuses. And filthy letters you wouldn't believe.'

But attacks can come from far more surprising sources. Even, I have to say, from those who claim to be one's Sisters. (I have only two half-sisters and rather resent anyone claiming to be my Sister; but then I'm the sort who, in the past, avoided going to church because of the distaste I had of shaking strangers' hands and saying: 'Peace be with you'. When I had to go, for weddings and Christenings, I tried to keep my hands in my pockets.) Anyway, one particular Sister wrote a paper for the British Sociological Society on 'Patriarchal Ideology and Agony Columns'. It was based on a 'study currently in progress' – so presumably there were people who were giving this topic more than just a passing glance.

Her basic complaint was summed up in an example:

> Because the agony column totally ignores the political context surrounding these choices [between having an illegitimate child and bringing up a child on one's own] it ends up condemning *them* [the mothers] rather than the social relations which are responsible for the circumstances. The agony column never asks why pre-marital intercourse leads to unwanted pregnancies and why single parenthood leads to financial hardship. These consequences are not inevitable but depend on the kind of society in which we live....

I had a rather touching letter from the sociologist after her paper had been turned into a *Daily Mail* story:

> I have no intention of making personal accusations against

agony columnists. I am not claiming that your answers are 'wrong' and that there are better (i.e. sociological feminist) solutions that you could give. What I *am* doing is looking at the agony column as a cultural artefact that expresses the views and values of the society in which it is made.... I may be critical of particular ideological meanings that the agony column carries but I recognize these meanings as coming from the society which produces them, not the particular individual who happens to hold the pen.... Best of wishes and In Sisterhood....

Cripes. Amazing what people can see in a simple agony column. Still, it was very decent of her to write in Sisterhood.

The Social Worker does not like my criticism of the Sister and shows it. 'I think if you met more of your readers in person you would realize what the sociologist was talking about,' she says. She has a point. I rarely meet the readers. But sometimes I do.

I'd never actually met any of my readers *en masse* until *Woman* magazine organized a joint venture with a big department store in the West End. It was a zany idea whereby we'd get the publicity and the store would get the customers. The idea was that the fashion editor would be featured in the fashion department, pinning up hems and suggesting chic accessories to readers; the hair and beauty girl would be in the make-up department covering up readers' spots and wrinkles; the cookery editor would be in the kitchen department, slicing up carrots and garlic and puffing up her pastry, or whatever; the home editor would be in the furniture and fabrics department advising on the colour of readers' curtains, and so on.

And at the top of an escalator on a landing, who should be stuck between Lingerie and Linens, sitting at a low coffee table with a pot of bubbling coffee beside her, but what Terry Wogan would, I'm sure, refer to as 'muggins here', under a wobbling sign which bore the words: 'Virginia Ironside Answers Your Problems ...'

At first no one came. I just sat there reading and re-reading my leaflets. Suddenly I knew what it must feel like to be Gypsy Petulengro when a freak thunderstorm envelops the end of Brighton pier. Nothing. No customers. But very slowly the clouds scudded away as over the loudspeaker came the announcements of who was where. I began to get the occasional customer. And customer was the word. They asked me the way to the fashion department and whether they could buy toile or voile there; they asked me what time the next free facials were starting in the beauty department. They asked me where the Ladies was and what time the store closed. They asked me if Haberdashery sold mending yarn or would that be Wools? They asked me where they could get a refund on damaged goods. But no one asked me about their problems. So far, so good.

But then word got about. A lady arrived and sat down, and I offered her a cup of coffee. It was scalding hot. I asked her what she wanted to discuss with me and she said it was the colour of the bridesmaids' dresses for her daughter's wedding. I told her that the fashion editor would be better equipped to advise – but she couldn't leave because she still had to finish her boiling coffee. We chatted about this and that for hours and, slowly, a queue built up.

I did have quite a few clients or customers or whatever you call them. But the fact that the coffee was still sizzling meant that each of them had to hang around for about twenty minutes before they could take their first sip. The queue started getting restless. I decided to take a break.

Backstage, in the offices, there was rumour of a drunken woman who was going round with her teenage daughter, creating havoc. I had an awful feeling that this was the one 'customer' who really was tailor-made for my little spot. And I really didn't want to meet her. I dreaded her arrival. I had a sandwich and went back. The queue had lengthened. Some real problems emerged. Slowly I managed to deal with all of them, feeling, finally, positively heady with kindness, sympathy and advice-giving. I could have done it all week.

Then suddenly there was a curious silence around me. Everyone's eyes were on a red-faced, aggressive woman tugging a gloomy-looking teenager, who pushed to the front of the queue. This, I knew by the all-too-familiar smell, was the drunk.

She sat down and breathed over me and asked me what she could do but she clearly had no intention of taking my advice. She'd been dried out, it turned out, several times, but she couldn't do without the booze. Eventually I got impatient and said what I had said to my mother several times in the past: 'Stop. Just stop. That's all you have to do.'

'But I can't ...' she wailed, reeling off a list of self-pitying and angry accusations.

'You can,' I said. 'I know people who've done it. Just stop.'

I thrust a leaflet into her hand. 'And what about your daughter?' I asked, looking at the sad and angry girl who clearly had been deputized to chaperone her on this trip. 'What do you feel about this?'

'I hate it,' she muttered.

'Well, did you know there are places you can go for help?' I said. 'Like Al-Ateen? Or Alcohol Concern?'

But the drunk had got up now and, grabbing her daughter's hand, reeled off. 'I don't want her to go to any of these places,' she said. 'I'm off. Fuck off.'

I felt dreadfully depressed after that and I still think of that poor girl. It was like seeing a beaten dog in Spain or a caged bird in China. I wished I could have done more for her. But then it wasn't she who had come to me for help.

Advising people by letter and on the page is a completely different task. I do think about my readers, I do worry about them and I do take their problems home with me. But at the end of the day we never meet, and I never see their tear-stained faces, their bruises or their haunted eyes. I don't have to take the same responsibility, in the end, as a counsellor in the flesh, and this gives my advice both strengths and drawbacks. Drawbacks in that I can only tackle the aspect of the problem they present in a letter, that I can't follow it up, that they get only one chance to speak; strengths in that this type of advice-giving gives me the chance to sum up their problem and to advise them in rather a tougher way than I might face to face. Certainly the replies given on the page are, like the letters, much edited and condensed versions of the longer personal letters each reader receives.

'But what I like is the satisfaction of hammering home a few basic points and hoping to get through to some women,' says Irma Kurtz. 'By the time the woman's problem gets printed it's usually six weeks later, so the chances I'm going to help a particular person in pain are very slight. But the aim on the page is to make a general point that will be of some interest to other women. What? Oh, that you're responsible for yourself, that you cannot expect anything to come from another person, not your happiness, that it can happen that you're happier with another person than without but you should learn to depend on yourself above all before you share. And that you should have something to share.

'I do tell people what to do but I always preface it by "If I were you", or "If I were in your situation". Anyone reading my page must get an idea of my general themes – that I don't hold with affairs with married men, I think fidelity is part of the deal, I don't believe we're here just to stroke ourselves, I believe that if we have children we have duties and responsibilities.

'And I'm damned if I'm going to tell anyone how to get a man away from his wife! He's made a contract with someone else, I don't see any reason he should get away!'

I hope, finally, that the page helps people generally as much as I help people individually by letter, in a different way. I hope that the information on the page helps people. I hope, too, that, in reading it week after week, some readers might, if nothing else, pick up a method of tackling a problem. In other words, I hope that the page teaches readers something. This sounds tremendously patronizing, but I'm taught daily by things I read – other people's problem pages for one, not to mention self-help books which, particularly ones from the States, frequently offer a wealth of good advice and strategies for dealing with life, relationships and feelings – and so I try to pass on what I've learned to the readers.

People are being taught a lot more than they think. Whenever I watch *East Enders* I'm aware that in many episodes the writers are doing exactly the same thing as agony columnists. The characters in it are forever sitting down and 'having it out' – just as agony aunts advise. Problems that come my way are constantly tackled: illegitimacy, rape, sexual abuse, Alzheimer's Disease – you name it, people in the soaps have lived through it and coped with it. Indeed, the soaps are the nearest that television has to problem pages, with dramatized methods of dealing with problems and even information about self-help groups frequently being popped in as the medicine in the jam.

People may read the problem page primarily for entertainment of one sort or another, but I hope that even if a reader never writes in, he or she will gain something more from the page than information, amusement and a warmed heart. I hope they'll learn how to look at problems. I don't mean to say that they should then necessarily follow the methods I suggest to deal with problems, but once you have a method at the back of your mind, a confidence that you know how problems could be tackled if you wished, then you can start to create your own to suit you.

*   *   *   *

Everyone is going now. Across the room, the baby is just starting to enjoy himself; it will be a long time before he gets to sleep. His first party. Held in his mother's arms, and admired by his adoring grandmother, he looks across the room bright-eyed and pink, his head wobbling slightly on an unstable neck. What are all these ridiculous people doing, he seems to be saying? And doesn't it all look just tremendous fun, whatever it is? This is my moment. The Social Worker has politely made her excuses and it seems that the Blazer and myself are among the last guests being swept up with the crumbs.

But just as I'm about to give my gift at last, the Blazer puts his face rather too close up to mine and says: 'Bet you get some really weird ones that don't go on the page, eh? One for the road? Eh? You've not got to drive. Come on!'

'Bet You Get Some Weird Ones ..!'

Every so often a letter arrives that makes my hair stand on end. It could be a letter about child cruelty, or one that reveals such intense misery that it makes you want to cry. These are the letters that you 'take home with you' in your head, the letters that worry you in the middle of the night.

What is more difficult is when the writers give their address and you know that a discreet phone-call to the right agencies would make matters a great deal better. I have only done this on about four occasions – and I know that some other agony aunts do the same. It's not a question, I feel, of 'Is it right to break the confidentiality of a letter?' It's a matter of 'Is it right not to?'

For instance, I once had a letter from a woman who had been convicted of arson. She had been put on probation and had got on very well with her probation officer. However, this man had left and a new one had taken his place, a man she had not met. She was becoming increasingly anxious. She wrote to me in despair saying that she had put barrels of paraffin in her attic and felt that pretty soon she would set fire to them. She was too nervous to approach her probation officer.

What would you do? Be confidential and let her burn herself and perhaps other innocent victims to death? I thought it over and decided I couldn't live with this knowledge without telling someone about it. Maybe I was kidding myself, but at the back of my mind I always feel that

155

if someone puts their name and address on their letter and tells me something perfectly frightful, some part of them is actually asking me to get help for them. This may well be a justification, but what the hell.

The result was that I tracked down the lady's new probation officer by ringing her local council, and he promised to visit the woman as soon as possible without telling her I'd called. Two days later he rang, thanking me very much for contacting him and said they had got on like a house on fire, if you'll excuse the expression, and everything was fine.

Claire Rayner only goes behind readers' backs in special cases. For instance, she once got a letter from a boy saying he was worried about his father. 'He was drinking too much. He was also an airline pilot. I called the British Airline Pilots Association to find out how likely the story was and they admitted unwillingly that there was a possibility because obviously pilots can have stress problems connected with the job. They gave me the name of a consultant in aeronautical medicine and he said yes it all sounded plausible. I gave him the name and address because I trusted him. He talked sense. And they did a snap, random health check on this guy which was quite common, and his problem was identified and as far as I know he was grounded....

'Then there was a man who wrote to me saying he was going to kill women and I thought, oh crumbs. Do you ignore it and say "Go to your doctor"? What do you do? I tracked down his GP through the local Family Practitioner Committee and contacted him outlining the problem and got a reply curtly saying: "If you're worried, call the police." Then I called the local psychiatric social worker and said: "Look, this is the story I've been told, I don't know if it's true but I'm worried, can you do a casual call?" and she did because he had a history of problems. They found he was going through a fairly florid phase of a severe mental illness, and he went to hospital and that was all I heard. I have called duty social workers often. I'll ring up and I'll say: "I've got someone on your patch here who I'm worried about. Is he or she known to you?" They often are. And the social worker will pop in. And with battered children I've often alerted social services, too.'

Claire also had a series of letters from a man who was a paedophile. He always gave a different address – usually of a motel – but it was always the same name and handwriting. 'I thought, if he is a threat to children he's going to go round playgrounds and so on, so I called the police – the only time I ever did – and the policewoman said she'd already had a call about a similar story from this man using a similar name. It was investigated and eventually he was tracked down. He was a salesman and they found a huge cache of pornographic photos of children. His story was that he was trying to uncover the Paedophile Information Exchange! He went to court. Originally I had written to him at each address saying: "Look, I'm going to call the police because I'm worried about this." And then I wrote again saying he should see a psychiatrist because either he was telling the truth, in which case a psychiatrist would help support him, or he wasn't so he'd got a problem and the psychiatrist would help him. Either way he'd get help. But he never answered.'

The other letters that have to be handled with kid gloves are the ones involving child cruelty. Obviously, it's very rare that anyone would write in saying they are ill-treating their child, at least giving an address, but sometimes someone will write in about a neighbour or a lover. Obviously, I will give them the address of the NSPCC, whose first step is always to come in and try to help the family through their difficulties first without taking the child into care, but as it's unlikely that anyone's going to get in touch I often end the letter by saying: 'What you say concerns me very much and quite honestly I won't sleep easily until I hear from you that you have contacted the NSPCC. If I don't hear back from you in three weeks, I will assume, by your silence, that you have no objection to my contacting them myself, without mentioning your name of course.' I have never heard back from anyone I've written to in this way – and have referred about four cases to the NSPCC.

Then a woman wrote to me in despair because her husband was constantly hitting their son in the face if he didn't do his homework properly. The first time she wrote she didn't give an address; the second time she not only gave her address but actually gave me the name of the school her son attended. The descriptions of the face-punchings and her son's permanent black eyes and his utter misery compelled me to ring the headmaster of the school. He confirmed that there was a problem with the family and assured me he'd look further into the matter. I never heard what happened.

Deidre Sanders of the *Sun* reacts similarly. 'Cases of child abuse are among the few where we intervene directly but discreetly,' she says. 'I've had letters from mothers worried about the degree of violence their husbands were showing the children. The husbands have usually threatened the wives with violence if they try to intervene. I can't safely even write back to the wives for fear of their husband intercepting the letter, but in cases like that I can't risk the wife not acting on advice printed in the paper – even assuming one could always include a reply in the paper, which I can't in every case. So in those cases I do get in touch with the local health visitor who can call round to see the children without exciting the husband's suspicions. The wife can just say: "Oh, the health visitor called round today." '

But Angela Willans disagrees. 'I think it would be impertinent to get in touch with the authorities behind someone's back,' she says. 'When I get a case of child cruelty I say to the parent that she must get help because *she* needs help, I wouldn't even say: "For the child's sake." I don't think that would work.'

Marje does not balk at intervention. When a desperate wife rang her from her home, having taken an overdose, she not only got the police and an ambulance to her but also arranged for her daughter to be collected from school to avoid submitting her to the horror of finding the home in a shambles and her mother fighting for her life in hospital.

When a woman wrote, worried about an elderly man who lurked about the park near a school who'd been offering the children sweets, Marje rang the police. They checked him out and found him harmless. And in the case of one boy, who wrote from a mental hospital saying he was going to kill himself because he was in love with a married male psychiatric nurse, Marje rang the hospital and talked to the boy's psychiatrist. From then on the psychiatrist vetted Marje's letters to the boy and between them they were able to get the boy better quicker than might be expected – because the boy confided so much more in Marje than in the psychiatrist.

Sometimes the police have contacted me. I once put an anonymous letter on the page at *Woman* from a girl who claimed that she had smothered and killed her baby deliberately in a fit of post-natal depression and felt dreadful about it:

The father of my baby left me for a 15-year-old girl. I had the baby, my lovely little girl, and loved her so much, but I loved her father as well and used to cry and cry. And my little girl looked so like this man. One day he rang up and said we might get together again, and I was so happy. But we had a row; he said the baby wasn't his – and the other girl appeared and shouted at me and I hit my boyfriend and he hit me and left me to walk five miles home. When I got back I didn't know what I was doing I was so upset. I went upstairs and smothered my baby to death. In the morning I heard screams from my mother who found the baby. They took her away and the coroner said she had died in her sleep. I cry every day and go to her grave asking her to forgive me. I long for her; all the time I picture her growing up. I am going to kill myself I feel so guilty. They say God is good and forgiving but he could never forgive me for what I've done. Why didn't they find out what I did? I wish they had.

The description of what had happened was so utterly authentic that I had no reason to believe it wasn't true. She gave me the date it had happened and said that it had been recorded as a cot death and she was tormented by guilt and anguish. She was in utter despair.

I had to put it on the page because there was no other way of getting hold of her. I suggested every source of help in the book, and begged her to confide either in her doctor or the Samaritans. I assured her that God forgave her and begged her to forgive herself. But I didn't recommend that she should go to her local police station and confess. I couldn't really see where this would get her.

Some reader obviously read the letter and felt I'd been remiss and contacted the police who subsequently left a message for me to ring them. I rang them back, and they said they'd be coming round to interview me and would like to see the letter. Did I have it? Unfortunately I did, and I told them so. I also had the envelope with a clear postmark on it and I told them that as well. (I wished I'd just lied, but I'm rotten at lying.) The appointment was made and I lay tossing and turning, imagining all kinds of dramas, with me refusing to give them the letter and ending up in jail for six months and so on. The thing was that it wouldn't have taken a Sherlock Holmes to trace this girl, by checking in the records for a cot death on the date she mentioned in the area she lived. Luckily, the date for the interview arrived and the police rang me to say that the officer couldn't come over because he had to appear in court and would ring me for another appointment. I heard no more from him. No doubt he'd felt the same way about the whole situation as me.

The other communication with the police was an even sadder call. A lady had written to me, suicidally depressed. 'Have you really thought about committing suicide as you said on your page?' she asked (I had mentioned the fact that week) and went on:

I have had these terrible thoughts for ages and I dare not tell anyone. I mentioned that you had said on your page that you had felt suicidal in the past to my mother-in-law who replied that 'People who do that are full of the devil.' I lost my father six months ago and it has had a terrible effect on me. I see life so differently now and most of the time I see sadness – people in wheelchairs, handicapped people, lonely old people. It's awful. I never used to be like this. On top of this my mother is very upset about it all and is completely dependent on me. Will this unhappiness ever go? I want to be as I was, a good mother and wife and confident in life.... I am sorry to ramble on. I suppose it was your answer to that lady that made me write. You look so absolutely normal and well adjusted, I just didn't think these thoughts happened to people like that. I suppose I am so frightened that I will not get better from this depression.

I replied personally to the letter, by return:

I am so very sorry to hear you're feeling so depressed. It's not uncommon for people to have suicidal thoughts. All kinds of people have had them, even happy-looking ones like me, and though I don't have them now I certainly looked very jolly to the outside world when inside I was so depressed.

It does seem almost certain that your depression stems from bereavement and the fact your mother is getting older and leaning on you. After all, when someone dear to you dies, you need people to lean on, yourself; you are not fit enough, emotionally, to cope with looking after her needs as well as your own. Six months is not a long time to suffer like this, either, and I assure you that time will heal everything eventually. I really do think it is your mother-in-law who is wicked to say such things about people are suffering so much with depression! You seem to have no one to look after you in this difficult time. No wonder you feel so dreadful.

I suggested she contact her doctor, ask at her local CAB for bereavement counselling, contact the Samaritans and sent her my leaflet on depression. I ended by reassuring her that everyone feels sadness all round them when they're depressed and said: 'Do write again. I feel so sorry you are feeling like this.'

But my letter did no good. The policeman was ringing to tell me that this woman had been found dead – she'd committed suicide – and there was no note. The only evidence that she'd even been depressed was the discovery of my letter back to her. They needed my letter for the inquest.

Deidre Sanders of the *Sun* had a terrible experience, in her early days as agony aunt. She received a tape-recording through the post, sent by a miner who had lost his job through ill-health. He hadn't been able to find another job, which had taken its toll on his marriage. His wife had left him, sued for divorce and he'd lost custody of their three children. The first weekend he had them to stay, he smothered them to death, tape-recorded his message to Deidre, posted it, then went home and shot himself. That must have been an awful message to receive – especially as there was absolutely nothing she could do.

The other letters that never see the light of day are the kinky ones. And the problem page does attract its fair share of eccentrics. Quite often I'll get a letter that appears perfectly normal on page one, slightly bizarre on page two, while page three finds the writer dressed up as a waitress with a nappy on – or similar peculiar gear – being forced to wait on three hulking men who are keeping him chained up day and night in a broom cupboard, or some such nightmare scenario. The first time I got one of these letters I was rather alarmed – but those who write this kind of letter rarely give their address and I guess they live in tidy flats and get a big thrill from writing down their fantasies and posting them off to me.

There are some who do put their addresses, however, and

want to meet me. One elderly man, a nudist, fell madly in love with me and begged me to meet him at a nudist beach in Brighton. He would be there waiting for me on Tuesday. I would recognize him by his enormous.... Needless to say I refused.

Early in my agony aunting days I had a letter from someone calling herself Mrs Smith, *a widow*, who was concerned that her son Malcolm was getting peculiar punishment at school. It seemed that the headmaster insisted on a 'tickling' detention – and there followed an extremely long and detailed description of what this involved.

'When the younger boys arrive they give their names and the offence committed and are properly marked down in a register. Having changed into PE strip, they stand in a row with their backs to the wall-bars, stretch their arms up and put their hands on a bar above their heads. When they're all like this, the tickling can begin. The prefect first runs his fingers lightly over the boy's chest, ribs and stomach, then he strokes his chest, and finally he tickles him again, this time more roughly....' She added: 'It isn't altogether healthy, not the kind of thing you want to be going on at your son's school.'

I agreed. It didn't sound at all nice. And because I was totally green, naive and thoroughly wet behind the ears, I actually wrote back and I suggested to Mrs Smith that I write a note to the boy's headmaster. I can't think why on earth I suggested it; I must have been mad. I would never dream of writing to anyone on anyone's behalf; even if someone writes asking if I could send a leaflet to a friend and gives the address I always refuse to do so. I send it to the person who wrote and ask them to hand it on.

Anyway, back to Mrs Smith. She wrote back by return of post; she was most enthusiastic about the idea. 'I am most grateful for your interest and concern,' she wrote, 'and I am inclined to think that a letter from you to the Headmaster would be a good idea to prompt him to take action. I enclose a stamped addressed envelope to him and would thank you again for your interest and willing. Here's hoping!' A stamped addressed envelope was included for a Mr Rust, Green School, 44 Freshfield Gardens.... Rather late in the day, I smelt a rat. It was the sae that did it. I checked with directory enquiries and found there was no such school. The address was a private house. So I just did nothing at all.

But three years later I got another letter, this time from a widow calling herself Mrs Rust. She complained that her son, Graham, was at a school where they practised a bizarre kind of tickling detention. Her address was 44 Freshfield Gardens....

By this time I had got my act rather more together. I fired off a cross note telling her to stop wasting my time when my department was so hard-pressed to answer genuinely urgent cases of unwanted pregnancies, suicides, depression and so on. I never heard from him (because I'm sure it was a him) again.

One of the most curious stories I was drawn into lay behind a letter that came from a man who was being blackmailed. It seemed he had put an ad in a men's magazine asking for a 'busty, black, oriental or Asian woman, for fun, sex and photos'. Only one person replied and said she'd never replied to anything like it before. She enclosed a topless picture of herself – and a box number. The man had given her his home address and his work phone number and a photo to show good faith. She then asked him to write an explicit letter saying what he'd like to do to her and what she could do to him – which he did. As far as I could gather, it all involved anal sex, sex toys, oral sex and watersports. After a while she suggested meeting at a hotel but said he'd have to send her the money for her to book a room. He said he couldn't afford it and the correspondence continued. Then she wrote to him saying: 'I'm sorry I will have to bring our relationship to an end because I have recently met and fallen for a man who was introduced to me through a mutual friend at a party. However, I also have to inform you that he is a freelance journalist who at this moment is compiling a report for publication. This report is about sexual deviances and perversions and will run over several weeks in the Sunday press. I've only told him brief details about you and he has offered me money for more detail. I feel that in my present financial circumstances I have no alternative but to co-operate with him.... I'm sorry to let you down like this.'

It was at this stage that he wrote to me, appalled, especially as he was a bachelor living at home with his elderly parents and they'd be shocked if they saw his photo and his fantasies spread over the Sunday papers.

I wrote back saying he should go to the police and there was no way any Sunday paper would be remotely interested in his fantasies – if journalists want to research sexual fantasies they have only to ring up a couple of the hundreds of doctors who are dying to get their names into the papers to find out fantasies more interesting by far than his. Easier still, they had only to ask around the office.

However, the police apparently weren't very interested and the next letter he had was from the 'journalist' who wrote an extremely unpleasant letter enclosing a sheet listing the details of the letters he held on file and so on, with my poor reader's address and phone number on it, plus a list of all the papers the journalist was supposed to work for, mainly tabloids. It all looked very credible to anyone not involved with newspapers. The list was labelled No. 148 so presumably there were other poor mugs being caught in this way.

After my recommending he still hold tight, the poor guy got a phone call from the man, who said that he was going to send copies of his letters to his elderly parents and his workplace unless he sent him money. Straight blackmail. Again, I said he should do nothing – and asked if he'd mind us investigating the affair since the blackmailer was giving an address. He gave permission but nothing came of the story –

and nothing came of the blackmail attempt except that apparently the Obscene Publications Squad rang our reader eventually, saying they'd arrested the man who had dossiers on fifty men. Lots of men had sent money for the hotel room, which they'd never got back.

I also get letters from people with problems that have got nothing to do with the page – they ask medical questions (I actually use a marvellous GP who replies to these herself), or ask if I can write speeches for the best man at a wedding. I'm asked beauty questions, fashion questions and a lot of legal and social security questions that really can only be answered face to face in conversation with either a solicitor or someone at the Citizens' Advice Bureau.

People regularly write in saying they met someone on holiday and want to get in touch, or, sometimes, they want to get in touch with people they haven't even met on holiday. 'At this Villa holiday I kept seeing this boy the other side of the pool. I think his name was Gary or Harry. He had light auburn hair and a twinkly smile and our eyes used to meet often. I know he liked me but we never spoke. When I heard him speaking to his mates he had a North Country accent. He wasn't on the same tour as us so I can't find his name out through them. Please help me. I think of him every day and I love him so much.'

Deidre Sanders of the *Sun* gets equally difficult requests: 'How long can I keep a tin of prunes?' asked a reader, and in the same post came a letter from a young man who believed he needed circumcision and wanted to know if he could get hold of a DIY kit to do it himself. 'One woman wrote about her accidental romance with her husband's best friend, saying, "We had an affair, but it wasn't international." And another chap wrote in complaining about "premature emancipation".'

Marje has been asked: 'We're coming to London next week. Can you suggest a show and a restaurant where we can take my mother?' or 'Where can I get clothes for extra-tall people?' She was even asked by one woman where she could 'get felt in Manchester'. Marje replied, 'You can get felt anywhere if you put your mind to it.' But she added a PS giving the name of a department store and advising the woman not to walk in saying: 'Where can I get felt here?'

I get quite a few letters from Nigeria, from people asking if they can marry me so they can come to England to continue their studies. But one of my oddest bizarre letters from Africa was from someone who asked if I could help her obtain three things. '1 A small axe, 2 A chocolate-making machine, 3 A shroud.' The mind boggles.

Another letter from Africa came from two orphans. Or were they orphans? The problem with these letters – and I get a regular number a year – is deciding whether they are professional begging letters or not. According to some rumours there are special agencies set up in Third World countries which simply churn out begging letters.

This one, however, particularly touched my heart and I put it on the page near Christmas. 'Please, please help us. We are two Ugandan children of 13 and 10 and our parents were killed trying to save their property in the war. We have no food or clothes except for what we stand up in and we are looked after by a dying old man. Please can you bring us to England to finish our education? Or send us food? I beg you from the bottom of my heart.' I felt terrible about that letter. Whether it was a professional begging letter or not, I'm sure there were many children whose description it fitted. I printed it and recommended that readers send donations in to Christian Aid.

As mentioned earlier, I get my fair share of letters from people who are mentally ill. They are certain that people are talking to them through their television sets, that their rooms are bugged, that the neighbours are listening in to their conversation. A typical one came from a friend of such a woman: 'The wife of our friend has become most peculiar. She says I'm having an affair with her husband – impossible because we live miles away. She also says she is having an affair with her neighbour, even though he is at sea. She says he flies back by magic at night and gets into her bed. Sometimes she roams the streets at night looking for this man. Her husband is very worried but says he won't tell the doctor because she seems all right at work. What should I do?'

Recently a psychiatric social worker kindly tipped me (and several other agony aunts) off that one of her patients was about to write to me and every other agony aunt to compare their answers. The letter we finally got ran into several thousands of words.

Some of the very mad letters have a certain odd poetry of their own. Like this one I got the other day with its curious spelling and punctuation:

I urgently desire the benefit of your considerable training knowledge and experience as an 'Agony Aunt' I am what is Termed through the Printed and Audial word 'A Herb' and an 'Urik' and would be so Personality as a natural Visually via 'Stage' Screen and Television. For even at a distance i radiate the atmodphare of Drunken' Pissing on the Floor of the Pub holding a Dish of Jellied Eels in One Tattoed Hand and a Muddy Football Boot in the other 'Tattoed Hand. I am never invited to a Home of the slightest Refinement of Breeding. And most emphatically certainly not to any White Home. Lord Lew Grade has recently teleqhoned me to declare that he can organize and orchestrate a Strategy with me with the 100% participation of Harold Wilson, President John Fitzgerald Kennedy Robert and Edward Kennedy The Kennedy Cabinet and Government. Whereby with the most revered and Respected I.Q. Brains at Harvard Yale Princeton together with the entire Priest Homosexual Prostitute Police Homosexual Prostitutes and Mass Media System of Homosexual Prostitute throughout the System of Planets Viz Venus, Aquarius, Neptune, Saturn Jupiter Mars, co-ordinated via International Gay Libs Prostitute Subdivision will be instructed the Grade Family Irish Catholic Wives to implement the most collosal and

Astronomical Campaign in Human History to emphatically
establish me as the most wanted House Guest plus 'Sage' 'Elder
Stateswoman' Deeply revered and Respected Authority Figure
in British High Society.

Would you please advise if in appreciation I should buy Viz
e.g. The Grade Wives a Crucifix, direct from Dublin, Eire and
Convert to Catholicism, act as Scotch and Irish Catholics and
Catholics in general Recommend the IQ Eggheads at Yale
Harvard and Princeton for the Brainpower Contribution as
Nobel Prize Nominations. Transmit a Thank you message to
the Priest and Police Homosexual Prostitutes on Venus Mars
Neptune Cancer Aquarius Jupiter etc. Or simply thank Lew
Grade and other Media Executive Homosexual Prostitute
Scarists Scriptwriters Producers Directors Actors etc. Please
advise.

Alas, poor Urik.

Claire has a regular correspondence with one King
George. 'He is a dear but completely and utterly barmy. He
writes saying: "Do not be shy about popping in and having
tea with me here in Deptford. Prince Wayne and Princess
Tracy would love to see you!" '

I've had letters from murderers, prisoners, relatives of
people in the news – and one of the few readers I got to know
quite well through letters actually made the headlines in a
tragic case.

I first heard from him about ten years ago. He was an
ex-policeman living abroad, who had recently broken up
with his wife. He was lonely. His letters were typed, highly
literate; he seemed exceptionally intelligent and well-read.
For some reason I started up a friendly correspondence with
him. I have since learnt never to enter into long
correspondences with readers, but I suppose I thought that as
he lived so far away there was never any chance of our
meeting.

I was surprised when I had a letter from him the following
year from England saying he had come over to look for

work. I replied in as helpful and friendly a way as I could. We continued to correspond. Some time later he went into a psychiatric hospital suffering from depression and we continued to write; then when he came out I had a call from our reception desk saying he was downstairs waiting to see me. I felt extremely nervous – not because his letters were anything but polite, amusing and friendly, but because I always have a slight fear of meeting readers, particularly male ones. But we had by now been corresponding for years, so I went down just to put a face to a name.

He turned out to be a huge, amiable man, a little edgy but with a good sense of humour.

The letters continued; he was in and out of psychiatric hospitals, then he got married but his wife left him shortly afterwards; then he rang me up from another hospital to tell me of a great plot the doctors had hatched against him and so on.

Eventually my partner suggested it might be wisest to stop corresponding with him. I didn't actually stop but I wound it down. The last I heard from him was that he had got married again and that his wife was expecting his baby. I wrote wishing him well.

I heard nothing of him for two years until I opened the pages of the *Sun* one day and saw this man's face staring out at me. Described as a 'wild-eyed genius', he had been sent to a maximum security hospital for pushing a young mother under the wheels of an express train. He was quoted as saying: 'I am being persecuted by hundreds of people. I don't know who they are or why they should be persecuting me like this. They want to make sure that someone dies. I don't understand it.'

I thought I had heard the last of him but recently I had a sad letter from him. He asked if I remembered him, he said he was well-treated but that he hardly associated with the other patients because 'they are either criminals or lunatics. I have no wish to have anything to do with men and women of either category. All those years ago it certainly never occurred to me that I would one day be ... with such people! With very best wishes to your family and colleagues. I have never forgotten your kindness to me, a complete stranger.' We still correspond spasmodically. It is not just the lives of others that have been touched by this tragedy; it is his as well.

Agony aunts themselves get paranoid – at least this one does. I am ex-directory, and I never talk to readers on the phone – I don't think it's my job and I don't think I'm good at it. I don't like answering the phone at work, not so much because of the maniacs who have rung in the past – only a few have – but I'm always uneasy about who might ring in the future.

Deidre Sanders of the *Sun* has much better reason to be paranoid than me, after a very dangerous brush with one of her readers. 'We had a chap who wrote in for a while who was very troubled sexually. He gave his address and we were writing to him for years. We got him seeing a psychiatrist, but of course he didn't tell the psychiatrist what his fantasies were. His letters then started to change. He demanded a bizarre sexual encounter with me. He could go to Soho and get anyone to do it for £25 but he obviously didn't want to do that. He then wrote and said that if I wouldn't, he'd come after me with an axe and a gun. Then he asked if I had any children, with the implication that he'd be after them too. That pressed all the buttons. So I phoned MIND to get their assessment on whether this was fantasy or whether I should take action and they said: "Ah yes, we would take action because he's threatening one of our therapists and we've already reported him to the police." It turned out that he'd been in Rampton previously and had attacked someone with a knife. After all this he got sent away to another secure hospital where as far as I know he still is. That was a lesson to me to keep my distance a little bit more.'

Every agony aunt is usually taught by some experience like this to be wary that some of the readers might be mentally unstable. The following letter shows that the anxiety is, I think, well-founded. It was received by an agony aunt colleague: 'I am writing to ask if you have anything to do with Virginia Ironside, if so show her this.

'Last week my wife left me for another man and took our two boys with her to East Anglia. She left a note saying "Don't bother trying to get custody of the boys. Read this...." And she left me the *Sunday Mirror* Virginia Ironside column with this letter in it.' It was a letter from a battered wife who had left her husband taking her children with her. She was worried that as she was now having an affair, her husband might be able to get custody. I replied that an affair wouldn't give him grounds for custody. He would have to show she was an unfit mother, that the children wanted to live with him, and so on, to get a case going.

I'm fifty [the letter continued], worked hard all my life, we have a lovely home, our boys are ten and twelve. I love my wife and thought she loved me. Now I've lost everything and will probably have to sell the house knowing these days the law is stacked in the women's favour. My wife may well have left me anyway. But I'm sure that after reading Virginia Ironside that made up her mind.

Virginia Ironside has solved my wife's problem, but it has certainly left me with one, don't you think? At present I'm not worried about bills, etc. I'm not bitter about the other man, I can probably get over my wife, I'll never get over my kids, but I will never forgive Virginia Ironside.

During my hours of insomnia, I have become bitter with women, I got to thinking that apart from childbirth, what contribution have women given this life of ours ... what Inventions, Discoveries, Medicine? But then again, they have introduced lying and conniving, when you consider the Holy Bible had to be rewritten to kid Joseph about the immaculate conception.

Now can you give me advice, please? Will the Court who gives my wife the custody of my kids, after her breaking a fucking commandment, be as lenient with me for breaking a commandment, by killing Virginia Ironside? Mark my words, I want a reply.

*   *   *   *

The Blazer finally looks around and then at his watch. 'Better get back,' he says. 'The old woman will be kicking up stink. Nice to meet you,' he adds. 'Cheers.' He shakes my hand.

I look around for the baby. I pass the Neighbour's Partner who is wearily emptying ashtrays, and tap my Neighbour on the shoulder.

'Oh, at last!' she says. 'I've seen you all evening but haven't had a chance....'

'Nor have I,' I say. 'I brought your little person this.' I wrestle in my bag for the teddy. 'He's gorgeous.'

Indeed he is. Leaning over his bald head and kissing his tender scalp I smell the lovely whiff of hot baby's skin mixed with Johnson's baby powder. It is a fresh, budding smell, quite unlike that of the rest of the room, and the sensation of his moist, fluffy scalp remains on my lips after I've kissed him.

'Oh, look what she's got for you!' says my Neighbour, handing the baby the teddy. 'Isn't that lovely!'

The baby reaches for it, clutches it, makes a dreadful face, hurls it on the floor and reaches up for my glasses.

'Oh dear!' says my Neighbour. 'What's the point? Still, it's the thought that counts. And thank you, anyway.'

'Thank you for the party,' I say. 'It's been fun.'

'See you,' she says. And I walk out into the cold, back home.

'So What's the Point?'

Agony aunts are a funny bunch. We are seen variously as eccentrics, do-gooding busybodies, enthusiastic, well-meaning amateurs, experts and, I often suspect, con-artists.

Marje Proops has always felt that agony aunts don't have a good image. We are, she argues, patronized and laughed at rather than taken seriously for all the work we do. She finds people she meets socially are first rather shocked at hearing what she does – particularly when she mentions sexual problems – and then, invariably, they nudge her in the ribs and chortle: 'You must get some very juicy letters, ho ho ho!' As soon as an agony aunt is recognized, advises Marje, she would be wise to protect her ribs.

But if any stranger so much as ventures an elbow near a rib, I get out an extremely long ladder and climb onto the highest horse I can find and give the questioner such an emotional doing over, such a tear-jerking performance (if necessary I don't hesitate to use the word 'God' which invariably stops them in their tracks, particularly as sometimes I mean it) that by the time I've finished with them the ones who never want to speak to me again are grateful to kiss the hem of my garment. Indeed, it does often occur to me, like Miss Lonelyhearts, that 'Christ was the answer, but, if he did not want to get sick, he had to stay away from the Christ business.'

If, however, you find the high horse attitude at odds with

175

the tone of what I've been saying so far, I can only describe my readers as like my closest relations. I can carp at them, I can laugh at them, I can moan about them, but that's because I'm close to them. If anyone else does the same, I close ranks and won't hear a word said against them.

On the other hand, we're not always very kind about ourselves. Anna Raeburn has been quoted as saying: 'I loathe the title of agony aunt. It gives you an image of a conservative lady in a crease-resistant frock and good shoes, and I've never felt like that in my life.'

And the press certainly does have a mixed view of us. Stephen Pile, the writer, loves us and thinks we are 'a band of people as near saintly as makes no difference ... violets upon the bogs and marshes of British journalism.'

Bernard Levin, when asking if Marje Proops did good, wrote: 'I cannot see how anybody ... can be in any doubt that she does an enormous amount, possibly – of direct, practical good, at any rate – more than any other single individual in the country.'

Julie Burchill, however, is not so generous. One of the many gripes she gave vent to in a piece in the *Sunday Times* was that we are, apparently, 'not favoured. Mother Nature was out on a picket line when the agony aunts got their turn at the cuteness counter. They are plain.' Worse still: 'The fact is that such agony aunts as exist these days (with the exception of the gracious, godlike Katie Boyle) are basically a Sex Thing; and like all public Sex Things, the agony aunt is a *bad thing*.' And finally, we dispense a 'cartload of clucking, smug, chuckling and nudge-nudge advice ... There is,' she concluded, 'just no excuse for them.'

How do you get to be an agony aunt? Most of us either fell into the job or were cajoled into it by desperate editors.

'When people write in asking me how they can be an agony aunt I always say, "If you want to be one, then you're not suited to the job," ' says Claire Rayner. 'I think you should always be dragged unwillingly into a job like this.

Other people should force you in. You shouldn't be after the glamour.'

Deidre Sanders went from answering consumer problems on *Woman's Own* to the agony column at the *Sun*. 'I get satisfaction from communicating complicated information in a straightforward way,' she says. 'It's a useful talent in our field. I'm good at digesting information and getting it across to other people in a way that makes sense to them. I enjoy being a helpful messenger, putting people in touch with things I think are going to be useful to them.'

Angela Willans moved into the agony world from a column on the *Daily Herald* which answered problems about taking the stains out of carpets and what to do if your baby was sick and so on.

Irma Kurtz got into it from being on a magazine and writing pieces like 'Sexual Jealousy – How Do You Cope', 'Marital Jealousy – How Do You Deal With It', and so on. 'I used to say I ought to write a column called "Speculum, the Way In",' she says. 'When *Cosmo* started, the editor noticed I had a knack with people's problems and asked if I wanted to do an agony column. It wasn't my idea. But the moment she said it I thought: "Yeah, because I'm bossy and I'm nosy, what could be better?" ' But she likes to keep agony aunting a second string rather than a career in itself. 'Ideally one shouldn't be paid for it at all,' she says.

Marje was a very reluctant comer to the agony column, being coerced into giving it a try by Hugh Cudlipp. 'You should never do this job for the money or the status,' she says. 'You have to feel deeply and always have an emotional response to every letter.'

Peggy Makins (Evelyn Home) only took on the job on condition it would be short-term until a replacement was found. The replacement never came. And Claire started when she took time off from nursing to look after her daughter. Having an opportunity to listen to *Woman's Hour* she thought: 'I can do that' and became a contributor. Later she was offered a column on mothercraft, as it was then called, on *Hers*, which developed into her first agony column.

'I have a strong puritan streak and a guilty conscience which makes me uneasy. I spent all those years being broke and suddenly to make a lot of money as a writer seemed very fortunate and I do think you have to pay your debts. If I wanted to make money I'd just write books because that's where the dosh is,' she says. 'But I like an agony column partly because I have an enormous curiosity. People are fascinating. You can't resist it. The day I see a pile of mail waiting to be sorted, I think "Mmm!" It's an agreeable task. And it's also agreeable to feel you're useful, and to be recognized as such.

'It's nice to be able to teach people and to be able to make people listen to one's views on, say, smacking their children. And I sometimes think if we've done nothing else, all of us, than stopping women from hitting their children when they wet the bed, that's enough.

'If we weren't there and everyone who wrote to us had to fall back on the NHS I honestly think the way the NHS is run now, that if all of us shut up shop, medical advisers included, the NHS wouldn't cope. They couldn't handle it. We cream off a hell of a lot of the work the welfare state ought to be doing. We do it for them.'

Every so often all the agony aunts (around thirty of us) have an opportunity to meet together for lunch. We get together about once a year, mainly because we do such a very peculiar job and there are so few people we can discuss it with. The conversation runs on the lines of: 'Is the Incest Crisis-Line still in existence?' 'What do you think of the Bristol Cancer Centre?' 'Have you read that marvellous book on confidence-building?' 'Did you hear the National Council for One-Parent Families is stopping/starting their helpline?' 'No, that abortion agency isn't an abortion agency at all. It's a pro-Life group in disguise.' And, of course, (in whispers)

'Did you see that absolutely *extraordinary* reply that X gave the other day on her page?' 'Oh, you put in for that job when X left. Well, er, so did I!' 'What about getting insured? The law is changing soon....' 'X must invent all her letters, surely!' and all the usual gossip.

We, as agony aunts, are by no means saints, and there's just as much gossip and bitchiness in the world of agony aunts as anywhere else. Some don't speak to each other, some speak to each other but hate each other; I remember feeling so slighted and hurt when Deidre Sanders and Claire Rayner, variously, were seconded on to *Woman* to write 'big features on sex and emotions' (I thought it was my patch) that I could barely speak their names let alone speak to them. Needless to say, the feelings passed. And yet there is a curious camaraderie about us. Suzy Hayman of *Essentials* writes a regular newsletter for us all to keep us up to date with new addresses, groups setting up or closing down, new books, ideas and so on. We are generous with our information and like to share it even with agony aunts on rival papers – because our first duty is towards our readers.

And, of course, readers' problems. You might think that because there are so many more avenues of help these days for people in trouble that our postbags would have decreased, putting us out of a job. 'But it seems to me there's an everlasting need to confide in the anonymous stranger,' says Deidre Sanders, 'and I can see that going on for ever and ever.'

I agree. There are always going to be people who like to write to problem pages because, sadly, there are always going to be problems.

After ten years of working at *Woman* and several years on the *Sunday Mirror*, it seems clear that although it is right that we continue to try to solve problems through legislation or through programmes set up to help specific groups of people, solving problems in itself creates problems.

For instance, think of the number of people in the past

who were trapped in incredibly unhappy marriages. It really was virtually impossible to get a divorce and many women – and, indeed, men – suffered miserably by having made the wrong choice in the first place. Women probably suffered more than men because men were given such a powerful position in the marriage, virtually owning the wife, her property and the children; and give anyone power and they often abuse it. But there must have been many men trapped with some dreadful nag, or someone who refused him sex or someone who took to her bed for years with nervous trouble and so on.

Now there is easier divorce to solve those problems – but although easier divorce helps thousands of couples who've made the wrong choice, it throws up all kinds of other problems in itself.

Divorce itself can result in incredible acrimony which can affect children horribly. Fathers lose access. Indeed fifty per cent of fathers who get divorced lose touch with their children completely. Easy divorce, some argue, means that fewer people work at their relationships in a way that they used to in the past; they throw in the towel quicker. From the letters I get I am not so sure that that is true – certainly the people who write to me often seem to be trying to keep their marriages together at a ridiculously high cost to themselves and sometimes their children, so great is their fear of being on their own.

But, whatever the reasons, the truth is that divorce can cause great unhappiness and not only unhappiness but confusion. My own son has one stepmother and one virtual stepfather; he has one grandmother, but three step-grandmothers, two grandfathers and one step-grandfather. He has a half-sister and two half-brothers, not to mention half-uncles and half-aunts. In his, as in many other children's, case, this diversity actually offers him an *embarras de richesse* in the way of relations and he considers himself incredibly lucky to possess this extraordinarily big family; but these complicated networks can cause terrible problems. Children do not always get on with their stepsiblings; it often isn't so much a problem of the nuclear family but the unclear family. And often it's not so much a case of the one-parent family but the four-parent family – dad's new wife and mum's new husband to be included. These complexities result in the most pathetic letters – the confusion often summed up in questions about where people should sit in church when a child gets married, who should give whom away, or whether it's right that the stepdaughter should be showered with gifts at Christmas from her mum when she goes to visit, when little Freddie, whose father has vanished, gets nothing from another family.

As far as relationships go, there's a new reality abroad. Out go the old fantasies about Mr or Miss Right getting married and walking hand in hand into the sunset to a rose-covered cottage to live in happiness for ever. What utter nonsense! Pure fantasy! We know better now. We've read lots of books, about psychology and relationships. But what have we established instead? We have established a new romance, an equally unattainable vision of relationships being shared partnerships, that he shares the housework and the cleaning, that she goes out to work, that they have a friendship rather than a love affair, that they are completely honest with each other, can always talk to each other openly about any problems, are frank and fearless about their sexual pasts ... all just as unrealistic as the rose-covered cottage idea. And the pursuit of which is just as likely to end in unhappiness.

Certainly it's a lovely fantasy; so is the rose-covered cottage. But it really isn't true for most people. Most couples rub along – and if they can do this with a minimum of rows and deceit and a maximum of shared fun and honesty, then that's a great relationship. As my father says: 'If a partner feels he or she is doing about seventy-five per cent of the work in a relationship then he or she is probably just about pulling their weight.' But the idea that marriage has to be this wonderful open partnership in which each has his or her own 'space' (whatever that may be) is not only piffle, but patronizing piffle. From the letters I've received I know that people put up with partners and relationships that I wouldn't put up with for five minutes – and no doubt they would not be able to put up with things that I find quite tolerable. But the fantasy lingers on, and sometimes people's expectations of marriage is not so much high as unrealistic.

A lot of the problems stem, still, of course, from the fact that women are not yet liberated. Women continue to write to me who have husbands of the 'stick to washing, ironing, scrubbing and cooking; no wife of mine is going to work' variety. True, the fact that women were completely unliberated in the past caused problems – but the transition from being unliberated to emancipated causes terrible problems too, not only for the mothers who often feel dreadful guilt about leaving their children in the care of strangers, but also the children who may feel miserable being left with child-minders. I was delighted to read recently of the pendulum perhaps swinging back again, in an article that argued vehemently against so-called 'quality time' with children, and for a return to 'quantity' time. But it'll swing the other way again.

In the past, sex was often a real problem. Women were not expected to enjoy it, they had often never seen men's genitals before getting married – were even from the tenderest age bathed separately from their brothers – and the constant fear of pregnancy sometimes played permanent havoc with their sex lives. If women slept with their partners before marriage in the past and didn't enjoy it, the agony aunt would all too frequently tell them that once they got married everything would be tickety-boo. 'It is only in marriage that the true union of two souls....' etc, etc. If they got pregnant, woe betide them. No wonder sex was a bit tense.

With exceptions, of course, those problems have been

largely removed by much improved contraception. The arrival of the Pill has indeed taken away the fear of pregnancy and made sex much more enjoyable for all. But the sting in its tail is that not only is there a wider spread of sexually transmitted disease, including AIDS, but also the expectation of greater fun from sex has bred its own problems. Women are so desperate for the mighty orgasms they read about in women's magazines that they often can't enjoy themselves in bed at all. It's a vicious circle, in other words.

In the past people died much younger than they did now and this in itself caused problems. There were motherless children, children forced to play parents to their orphan siblings, misery caused by illness and stress, and anguish caused by frequent deaths. Nowadays, however, people live very long – and this in itself causes problems. In the past you might not have been expected to live with your partner for more than perhaps fifteen years. One of you would have popped off by then. But these days with your life expectancy so much greater, you may live together for thirty, forty or sometimes fifty years. It is very hard to get along with someone else for that amount of time, since people do change with age and you can't always guarantee you're going to change in the same direction. Not only that, but we are now faced with the problem of our old relations – our old parents in particular. Which throws up all those problems of whether to give up years of one's life to care for a perhaps incontinent and senile mother who is quite unlike the person you once knew and loved, or whether to put her into a home.

In the past, problems arose from overcrowding. Several families might live in one room – and indeed up to a point this problem still exists today. But a problem that didn't exist in the past, I'm sure, was the isolation of a lonely bed-sit. I am inundated by letters from lonely people who live by themselves, a problem not found in the problem pages of the past. But the past was perhaps harder than it is today. It was, for most families, a case of all work and no play. Holidays were a rare luxury and holidays abroad almost unheard of. There was a lot more poverty around than there is today, despite the current situation. On the other hand, today there is perhaps too much leisure, the horrible enforced leisure brought on by unemployment.

As poverty was rife, so luxuries could not be afforded. Many people were glad to get enough to eat. I know that cases of anorexia have been recorded among the ancient Greeks but I wonder how many were recorded, say, seventy years ago? The whole area of dieting is a comparatively new one and one that has come immediately on the heels of everyone having enough to eat. And with dieting come other problems, like bulimia, the all-too-common syndrome where people gorge themselves on food and then force themselves to sick it up, usually using a dangerous amount of laxatives at the same time.

A hundred years ago it was much less easy to travel than it is today. And if you were stuck in a village where everyone had got married off except you, your prospects might not look too rosy. You would in fact, have a problem. You might even write to a problem page.

Today, we can travel far and wide and if no one's left in the village at home, then what about the big city? Or what about marrying someone from another country? How about an Arab, someone with totally different customs and laws to our own? Yes – you guessed it. More problems. She finds her husband expects a wife of a very different kind from the one she is prepared to be. This is not his fault, or hers. It's a sad side-effect of a greater ease in travelling from country to country, widening our horizons and opening us to foreign ideas and mores.

And what about if you are from a different culture and come over here for a happier, less problem-filled existence? Obviously it often works out – but not if you're an Asian girl brought up in an English school among English people who

suddenly has to submit to an arranged marriage to someone
from a remote village in Pakistan.

What of medical help? In the past there really wasn't a lot
of it about. It was either an aspirin, leeches, a hot flannel or
cod-liver oil. Today there is far greater scope for help, with
new drugs and new operations developing by the minute. But
there isn't enough money for everyone to have them –
problem No. 1. And there seems to be a growing
expectation, among some of my readers, that doctors are
absolute gods who ought to be able to do anything. '*Why*
can't the doctors come up with anything better than the Pill?'
whines one. '*Why* can't he do anything about my anxiety
attacks?' Or, more sadly, a cry from a lady who had had a
total hysterectomy and wanted more children. 'Surely,' she
wrote, 'surely there is *something* these doctors can do to
make it possible?'

Medical problems seem to be on the increase as well,
mainly because the doctors have discovered more things
wrong with us. Ever heard of PMS in 1920? I doubt it,
somehow. Certainly it wasn't known to the extent it is today.
Some have argued that since women had more children then
and breast-fed for longer, that the problem didn't really
manifest itself until women had far fewer children and had
long stretches when they could start to be aware of their
cycles in a way that their grandparents could not.

In the past people were, it is true, often trapped by terribly
rigid religious ideas. This made some of them extremely
uncomfortable and guilty a lot of the time and many were
tormented with anxiety about hellfire. But, on the other
hand, it gave others an inner treasury of security, a security
few people have today.

I am very aware, too, of how many people today are
troubled by great fears – of death, chemical warfare,
over-population, a dying environment and so on. Mothers,
particularly, are often haunted by fears of nuclear war when
they have their first children. What kind of world are they

bringing them into? And it is this change of future that has been responsible for the so-called generation gap. In the past, your mother's and father's past would have been very similar to your own. They would have had exactly the same financial, social and sexual fears as you. Today, the young are dealing with entirely new problems that their parents often simply can't understand because they have had no experience of them. The young have different expectations, as well, and, often, different values. As the French poet and philosopher Paul Valéry said, 'The trouble with our times is that the future is not what it used to be.'

It often seems to me that there is simply a cloud of gloom above the world that can never be dispersed; all that happens is that it is shoved around from time to time so that the rain falls on different members of our society. Laws are passed to make homosexuality and abortion easier; so some groups have an easier time than in the past. But conversely, more people's lives are ruined by drink and drugs than in the past, and with material expectations so high – since everyone can see them on the telly (which is a great comfort to lonely people) – perhaps more people feel cheated and disappointed. And so on.

We're never going to run out of problems, that's for sure. If it's not the whole area of genetic engineering, including cloning, AID, choosing your children's sex and so on, it's new diseases like AIDS. If it's not races being discriminated against, it's indigenous races feeling their rights are lost. It's swings and roundabouts. And the role of the agony aunt will never, I fear, be redundant.

Problems have not changed much over the years that I've been an agony aunt. The big changes came in the early sixties and seventies; since then problems have been much the same, with only slight variations. And, anyway, when you read the letters, it's not the problems that are as important as the feelings behind them.

Marje has written: 'We will always be a joke. But no point

in whingeing about it. Who cares, really, as long as our readers continue to take us seriously and we are around when someone writes: "I'm desperate and I don't know what to do or where to turn. Please, please help me...." '

Whether it's shed by a man in a wig and a frock-coat or a woman with spiked hair and a mini-skirt, a tear is still a tear. Sorrow never changes. But at the same time, whether it's offered as a linen kerchief or a Kleenex, comfort is still comfort. Whether the advice is right or wrong is, perhaps, beside the point. And God knows, we've all got things wrong. But the point is the feeling with which the advice is given. Love and kindness do matter.

Corny, I know, but true.

On Another's Sorrow

Can I see another's woe,
And not be in sorrow too?
Can I see another's grief,
And not seek for kind relief?

Can I see a falling tear,
And not feel my sorrow's share?
Can a father see his child
Weep, nor be with sorrow fill'd?

Can a mother sit and hear
An infant groan, an infant fear?
No, no! never can it be!
Never, never can it be!

And can He who smiles on all
Hear the wren with sorrows small,
Hear the small bird's grief and care,
Hear the woes that infants bear,

And not sit beside the nest,
Pouring pity in their breast;
And not sit the cradle near,
Weeping tear on infant's tear;

And not sit both night and day,
Wiping all our tears away?
O! no never can it be!
Never, never can it be!

He doth give His joy to all;
He becomes an infant small;
He becomes a man of woe;
He doth feel the sorrow too.

Think not thou canst sigh a sigh
And thy maker is not by;
Think not thou canst weep a tear
And thy maker is not near.

O! He gives to us His joy
That our grief He may destroy;
Till our grief is fled and gone
He doth sit by us and moan.

William Blake